CARRYING FIRE
AND WATER

DEIRDRE SHANAHAN has published stories in several journals including *The Southern Review*, *The Massachusetts Review*, and *The Lonely Crowd*. Her work was included in *The Best of British Short Stories 2017* from Salt and, in 2018, she won the Wasafiri International Fiction Award. She is also the recipient of an Arts Council England award for her writing. Her first novel, *Caravan of the Lost and Left Behind*, was published by Bluemoose Books in 2019.

D1612335

First published in paperback in 2020 by Splice,
48 Milner Road, Birmingham B29 7RQ.

The right of Deirdre Shanahan to be identified as the author of
this work has been asserted in accordance with
Section 77 of the Copyright, Designs and Patents Act 1988.

Paperback Edition: ISBN 978-1-9161730-3-3
Ebook Edition: ISBN 978-1-9161730-4-0

Cover Design: Terriana/AdobeStock

CARRYING FIRE AND WATER

Deirdre Shanahan

ThisIsSplice.co.uk

In memory of my father,
whose stories paved the way.

Contents

Carrying Fire and Water

WE STAYED AT THE CASPIAN HOTEL because it was in the old city. I stood on the balcony while Richard dozed on the bed. He draped his limbs over the edge like an exhausted athlete, even though we hadn't been anywhere but down to the beach and back to the hotel to dress for the evening. Little boys in white robes with red capes and hats paraded before their circumcisions. Running alongside them in the street was the small boy I'd seen on the first day, at the fruit stall. As we'd passed under the awnings and made our way through the crowd, I'd suggested to Richard we should buy some grapes.

We're not allowed to, he said and walked on.

I looked over my shoulder, picking up my pace to match his stride.

Nobody will know, I said.

The maid will, when she sees the stalks.

I'll flush them down the loo.

You can't. It gets blocked as it is.

In my bag, then. I'll dump them in the morning.

AFTER THE FIRST TIME, it was easy. I found an excuse to stop at the stall every day, maybe twice. The little boy who served there had eager eyes and perfect olive skin. He'd examine the balance, which was as tall as he was, and tuck down the edges of the paper bag.

Thank you, madam.

He had an ease, a repose, against the clatter of the street. The afternoon air had been light and the colour of honey as he handed over the packages of apples and grapes. On the cart, in greaseproof paper, lay slices of cake. Fragments of sugar glistened beside a huge slice of watermelon which wept as flies settled on it. Richard had bought the most delicious pastries after the results came back. Perhaps this was why I liked them, because at the time I had been in low spirits.

He'd set his briefcase on the hall table without taking his eyes from me.

Is something wrong, Marie?

No. I shook my head. No, nothing. But.

But what?

It's negative.

He stared at me and gave a single, sober nod.

They're sure? he asked.

Pretty sure.

Richard turned aside and began unknotting his tie. Never mind, he said. Really. We have each other. We'll have money to spend, this way. We can afford to dip into our savings, splash out on other things. It's simpler, this way. What would you like?

I followed him into the dining room where he laid his tie over the back of a chair and shrugged off his jacket.

Nothing, I said.

He draped the jacket over the tie and sunk into the chair.

We could travel. Get a new car. Or do both. The Citroën takes up so much room in the garage.

It's comfortable.

We can downsize, though.

That'd mean less power.

It doesn't have to. Go to the garage around the corner. They have a good stock. You might find one while I'm away.

I'D WALKED THROUGH rows of cars. The salesman stood tall among the fleet. He was bony around the face, as if he hadn't eaten for weeks, and he wore his name on a large badge: ASHOK. SALESMAN OF THE MONTH.

This is Atlantic Blue, he said. Or there's Diamond White and Mercury Grey.

Could I try this one?

I lay a hand on the bonnet of the silver car.

He got inside to key the engine but he couldn't start it.

Don't worry, I said. I'm not put off.

It's probably no petrol.

He had a way of phrasing I liked.

This one has a headrest so if you're thrown forward like in an accident, the head is supported.

He demonstrated.

I would say even if you do not buy this car, make sure the one you do buy has a headrest.

His eyes were dark as plums.

My sister was saved by the headrest when she had an accident, so I know it is important.

He led the way from the cushioned interior of a Fiesta to a Verona.

LEAVING RICHARD IN THE HOTEL, I stopped at the fruit cart to buy figs. A gaggle of boys trailed after me. They used to hang around on the corner near the tobacconist when they left the hotel in the mornings.

Chanel Number 5, said one.

Opium, chimed another.

No thanks.

Postcards. Chanel Number 5.

No.

The boy from the fruit cart ran towards us. He shouted at the other boys and stamped a foot. He waved his arms and the others ran off.

Tesekkur ederim was all I could say. But my scarf had gone, dropped in the rush. Never mind. It was only a scarf. I searched my purse for change. But the next evening, after touring the back-streets, I stopped again at the fruit cart and the boy thrust my scarf towards me. Swirls and waves dropped from his palm.

Oh, I said. Thank you.

He bowed to his dusty feet. Dark hair fell over his ears. He was only waist-high. I could have hugged him in relief because I could still hear Richard's admonitions. You're so casual. You're careless with things. You always lose them.

Further down the street, a dark limousine crawled up to park in front of the leather factory. Wing mirrors caught the sun even though the light was weakening. A young man nipped out and opened a door at the back to allow the sweeping passage of a man in a long robe. The man entered a restaurant with a flutter of his tunic, and the car hummed off. Ashok would have liked the car. Not Richard. It was too old for him.

I had kept going back to the showroom.

THIS IS THE HEADLIGHTS, fog lights and heater. Here's the back wiper.

Does it warm up, the rear window?

Of course. Look at the lines. If you would like a test drive? This car is for you? For work?

Sort of. I work from home.

You have a lot of things to put in the boot?

Yes, exactly why I need a hatchback.

You can lie down the back seat. See?

Ashok repositioned the seat. We walked on to look at other makes, other models. In a low red car he switched on the radio.

The slick ease of a trombone came stunningly to a shimmering conclusion.

It is good to have music in the background. But I know what we should do.

His eyes held me darkly.

Come to my place. It is near.

He put out his hand towards mine, gathered it into his.

We walked together. His shoulderblades were visible beneath his light shirt. His flat was in one of the ugliest buildings I'd seen in Enfield. Derelict garages and patchwork gardens surrounded dull cement blocks with no windows.

I was lucky to find this place from a guy at work, said Ashok. I had nowhere when I came over.

He possessed all the assuredness of someone young, someone who knew life could only get better. Asleep beside me, he turned to rest his face on his arm with the ease of a child. Tiny wrinkles at the corners of his eyes disappeared as if he had no worries, as if he had not known war.

I will get my mother out, he told me once. She did so much to get me here. Used all her savings to buy me a ticket. She works as a cleaner. I try to help. She lost her house and lives in a room in the city. No water but she wants to stay. I send her money when I can but she doesn't like it. She is a woman who can carry fire and water.

What was it like to have such a mother? To be loved so much by a son? They were separated but not by distance. A bond kept them close. But Richard was due back after four weeks abroad. I had to tell Ashok we could not go on. It was not serious. I had only liked him and the cars.

I can't see you again, I said.

He frowned, his arm propping up his head as he leaned in towards me.

I'm going away, I said.

Away? To where?

Leaving England. To work abroad.

Where to?

I didn't tell him. I told him not to think about it. You'll forget me, I thought. In a few weeks, I'll be nothing. I am nothing. I couldn't even give you a child if you wanted. What would your mother say?

RICHARD LAY ON HIS SIDE. He drew his knees up to his stomach as if this position might dispel the diarrhoea.

How do you eat all the pastry? he asked. You must have a cast iron stomach.

It's the ancestry. In Donegal they were grateful for anything to eat.

In the morning I gave the surplus figs to the maid while Richard shaved. In the afternoon I leant against the Venetian blinds and felt the heat fading behind me.

Ismail! a voice roared from below. Ismail!

I turned and looked out at the street. The boy cowered under a blow from an old man. Oranges rolled across the ground, bright as boiled sweets. The boy ran into a doorway and took refuge there. He sat on a wooden crate, crying. I knew he was crying, even though I could not see him anymore, because if he had been mine he would have cried. I turned to Richard on the bed. A child somewhere wanted a home, needed what we could give. I pushed open the window. Traffic murmured while pop music from the record shop hurled itself at me. I couldn't see Ismail. The cart and the old man had gone. I wanted to shout to the pedestrians and ask if they had seen him. I could run down the street but there was no point and I had no right.

IN THE EVENING we ate at the Topkapı. I sat facing the pavement. Lumbering cars from the nineteen fifties rolled by, fat and bulbous as the old men gathered in the cafés. In England, Ashok might still be at the garage, though people who deal in cars often move around. A dark red saloon slowed at the lights. I saw the boy in the back. Ismail. The lights turned green and the car surged off.

Did you decide while I was away? Richard bent towards the salt and pepper.

About a child?

His eyes rested sharply on me. About a car, he said.

Oh. Not really. I looked around but I couldn't choose.

Ashok came to me. The spread of his thin arms behind his head as he rested back against the pillow.

A Peugeot would suit you, Richard said. The new 300. You should try it. Our press officer found one and it's only a year old. She really likes it.

He raised his glass and sipped his wine. Beyond him rose a delicate minaret. The evening hummed with the dust of the streets and the sellers, the little boys dodging between stalls as they ran, and coils of music looping through the dry air.

Orphanages? I said and put down my knife.

What? He held aloft a spoonful of aubergines dripping their tomato glaze.

I shook my head. Oh, I said, a new car. All right.

Oils from the rabbit stew smeared my plate. Bits of gristle and skin dragged around the rim. Beyond the window, past the other diners, the Bosphorus caught the bracelet of lights from the cafés along the terrace. The reflections dazzled the water's surface. I wanted to rush to the ladies' room, but I held my breath. I could do this. I could sit with my husband at a table with an immaculate white cloth, waiting for our desserts.

The Beach on Silhouette Island

AFTER THE NURSE HAD BEEN IN, Catherine went up to see her father. More times than she could count she'd climbed the stairs to his room overlooking the sea, chosen because he liked to hear gulls and smell the salt in the air. He lay against the pillow with his glasses off and his teeth in a saucer on the bedside table. His skin was unwrinkled, soft like a child's, one of the few things of which he was proud. Because I use palm olive soap, he used to say, to annoy his wife while she was alive.

He turned to face Catherine when he sensed her presence at the door. Ah, he said. I thought you were the old girl, Maguire. Have ye bought me any baccy?

You know you're not allowed it.

Ah, I'll never have a puff again. And there's nothing to do here.

He spread out his arms against the sheets. Catherine took the empty seat beside the bed.

You could listen to the radio.

My left ear's going deaf.

Read the papers, then. She moved the newspapers from the end of the bed, nearer to him.

I hate them. The ink comes off on my hands. Haven't you any little thing of your own to show me? He shifted around in the bed, as if he'd give anything to be out of it.

I'll bring something next time.

The pad of drawings lay on her sofa at home where she had been looking at them and where she wanted them to stay. Sketches of Carson before he'd left. She didn't want to carry them around like old memories. She had enough of those. She'd been trying to capture difficult dark tones, the places on his throat where his skin became almost milky, at those times when his jet eyes could look fearful and sad at once. She'd spent hours smoothing lines on the creamy paper, letting her crayon follow the grain. If only the lines could come to a kind of life, capture him as truly as she'd once held him, cradling his head, stroking his rough hair after they'd made love, when she was slow and dizzy with excitement. She brushed her index finger over his wide cheekbones, carefully defining his face.

A shame your mother can't see them, he coughed, jerking up against the sheets. She would've liked to.

The words hung between them. Her mother had always been enthusiastic about Catherine's painting, even when she did not understand it. She had stood in front of several large canvases of colours in irregular shapes, shaking her head but not criticising. He lay back with his cheek to the pillow, like a baby in a great calm with the faint bellow of the waves below. Him. Her. And the waves. All that was left after the summer before, when she had turned to them as a kind of refuge after the break with Carson and joined them at their cottage on the coast of Kerry.

SHE HAD WALKED ALONG THE SHORE, up and down the rocks, after a breakfast of thick bread and butter with salt sharp as sea spray. She wanted to be alone, to find company in the boulders. A pool held a clump of oyster shells with deep silver interiors like fish scales. The sea crinkled into a blister, rare for the time of year. Waves pounded the sand and fell away with open arms.

Where've you been, dear? Her mother came up beside her, hot and out of breath. She had a strained look to her face and raised a hand to her hair, catching the trails of flour in her curls. Won't you come in for your breakfast? It's chilly and you haven't a cardigan on. You'll get a cold like your father. Her voice had risen and sunk with the waves.

Catherine had stayed on the rocks until her cheeks were chilled. Dammit she would get her work the way she wanted it; the exact shape of the ridge and the peculiar light. Being by the sea was exhilarating and had opened up her senses like a first rush of pleasure. Her mother's demands were irritants. Why couldn't she let her work? There must be plenty to occupy her in the house or the village. It had been her idea, after all, to visit the site of her girlhood and seek out old friends from over fifty years before. She'd never understood her daughter's sketching. Scribbling, she called it, even on holiday.

But I have to, Catherine said. To keep alert, alive to what's around me.

Her mother stopped in the midst of a field.

Can't you have a rest for a day or so? All the close work can't be good for your eyes.

I have to get this done.

You want to be careful, said her mother. You'll be washed away. She patted down her long apron and returned to the house.

CATHERINE ROSE FROM THE CHAIR beside her father's bed. His watery eyes were open.

You never came to see her much, he said.

Oh, Dad.

Your mother asked for you, at the end. You were all she had. Not like her sister, with the half-dozen of them running around.

I was travelling.

You were always off.

I'm back now.

You'll be off again soon. Why did you go such a long way?

Carson wanted to see where his family came from.

A shame you weren't at that place when I rang. You said you would be.

I couldn't help it. He wanted to go somewhere different.

Which one was he, anyway?

The one who had the studio next to mine.

Ah, he said. That fella. What happened to him? How is it you didn't make a match?

He went away. We broke up.

You're old enough to know your own mind. We can't keep tabs on you anymore.

And they couldn't. Somehow, she knew, she was never around. At Christmas she'd been in India; at Easter, in Senegal. She had spent her father's last birthday in Mexico driving through scrubby villages with shacks and chickens and women in black who looked for all the world, except their tans, as if they might have belonged in the extreme west of the Kerry she remembered from her youth. She was always travelling from one place to the next, always away, at one end of the earth when she should have been at the other. And travelling and art were the twin attractions of Carson. He had combined a love of both and in himself was like the two, either on the move, quick, agile and fleet, or quiet and at rest, totally absorbed in his work.

She had walked through the woodyard with him in Chiswick, as he told her about the varieties of veneers and grains he was considering for his next sculpture. He had got to know the manager and worked out good deals for off-cuts, odds and ends which couldn't be sold otherwise. She liked him better this way, when he wasn't working and so obsessive about time he never wanted to go out. Throughout the winter he had stayed many nights in the studio. He hadn't even headed home to her, but settled for a few hours sleep between two and six before setting to work again.

Slaves, he told her. But different from Michaelangelo's.

When he finished, it was he who suggested they go away.

I need to live a bit, so I have something else to put into my work. What about a week in Italy?

I can't. My mother. She's not well. I haven't seen her for a while. I'd like to go over.

You don't usually.

I have to this time.

Why don't you go this week, when I'm in Birmingham?

She'll be out of hospital later and will need me.

Go, if you want, he'd said in a hurt, childlike voice.

She is my mother.

Okay. He strolled off into the next aisle of wood with his hands in his pockets.

Damn him, she'd thought. Why does he have to be like this? When I need him.

It's all right, Catherine said. We can put it off for another time. It's only France. We can go somewhere else, somewhere really exotic.

THEY LEFT IN JUNE for Morocco, then Egypt, and on to Kenya. At the east coast, as they'd started to run out of time, he'd wanted to go directly to Silhouette Island. She'd watched him lying back against the whiteness of the fine sand.

The shoreline's so straight, she said. It goes on and on.

Crazy, isn't it? He moved close. Mmm. You smell nice. The sea.

Diorissima, she said.

He laughed, encircling her with his arms, flecks of sand on his legs and the pinky brown soles of his feet.

What's the matter? he said. Don't you want to?

Here?

Why not?

I feel, she began. But she didn't finish and twisted away.

What?

Nothing. Not now.

Please yourself. He rolled off.

A gutful of emptiness rose in her. Usually she loved the secrets and tricks his hands played on her.

He stood up and said, I'm going for a walk.

He strode off: a tall, dark shape like an arrow piercing the horizon. She watched as if she could not run after him. Afterwards, as she turned the pages of her book, she felt as if he was beside her. As if he was the quietness. She looked again and saw him way out near the crush of waves, gazing out to sea as if the future was on the horizon and was one which was not with her.

She sat on the terrace at the back of the cottage, sketching. The day was light and without a breeze. She'd risen early to complete this set of sketches, preparatory work for when she got back.

You'll strain your eyes, Catherine, her mother had said from the kitchen door.

I want to get this before the weather changes.

Her mother came up close, looking over her shoulder.

What is it? she asked, taking off her glasses.

A man.

What part of him? He has no eyes.

His back, Catherine said.

He's a big bulk of a fella and isn't he dark?

Catherine looked up. Her mother swayed from side to side.

Are you all right? Catherine asked.

It's the heat, I expect. There hasn't been a good summer like this in years.

Her mother fell exhausted into a chair, glasses in hand. She looked frayed and tired. Her skin was thin and loose. Catherine wanted to embrace her, hug her into rejuvenation, make her into the resilient woman she'd known when growing up.

I think I'll lie down.

Catherine held her mother round the waist and took her upstairs, going slowly so her mother did not falter, until she stopped.

But your father will be back at lunchtime and he'll want something to eat.

He can sort it out.

No, he can't. He never could manage without me.

You've spoilt him over the years, Mum.

I have. But what's the use of thinking on it? He's a good man and he likes his food. Where was I?

You were saying you'd lie down. Come on. Catherine guided her into her bedroom, to lie on top of the eiderdown, so her once pretty face was painfully visible with all its creases.

I wish you were married. Settled and secure.

Oh, God.

What, dear?

Her mother was trying to get up from the bed, the hem of her dress rising to show the tops of her stockings and her white slip. Her hair was thinner and her dress sagged around her waist where it had once fallen from a full bosom. When night arrived, with her breath barely audible as she slept, she moved ever so slightly as if in a difficult dream.

Catherine?

Yes?

Ah, you're there.

Of course. How do you feel?

I've still the pain. What's that noise?

The wind.

Are you sure? So strong. I feel as if this place will be blown away.

Of course not. How could it?

Didn't they have hurricanes in America last year?

They always do.

Ah, but those ones were worse than ever. Those poor people having their homes swept away. In the end, all a person has, is her home.

THEY HAD BEEN ON Silhouette Island for six days when her father had phoned with the news about her mother. She would never forget the day because of the dogs. On the white beach a yelp broke the silence. A lean grey dog trotted up to another straggly black one a few yards ahead. A shift from foot to foot. The dark one moved away. Glassy eyed with fear, showing his greasy teeth. His stocky legs slipped beneath him. He skidded on the sand and collapsed. The grey dog leapt onto his back. Catherine watched in strange fascination. The grey dog clawed his opponent. With his paws he gripped the other dog's sides and hurled him over with spirited kicks. Tufts of hair flew everywhere. The graze of muscle and feet. Ears sharpening. Blood trickled down the black dog's leg as a fleshy wound opened up. The grey dog ran off, up the beach, into stray grasses.

Catherine was nauseous as she watched the injured animal stumble away, dragging the leg splashed with scarlet. She wanted to rush forward and pick it up, but she knew it was no good. It limped back to the main road. When it was out of sight Catherine sat waiting for Carson to come back with the drinks. He was brighter and she was pleased.

Are you all right? he asked.

I was thinking about my mother. How time passes.

You worry about her too much. There's no point. She's had her life. You've got yours. Live it. I'm sorry about earlier on. I was a bit of an arsehole. Do you want to go in?

So they did. And when they made love it was easier. She wanted to hold him close for hours. Alarmed at her sense of loss, haunted by lingering images of the violence between the dogs, she hungered for his comfort.

WHEN THEY ARRIVED HOME to a rainy November, Carson mooched around the flat for hours.

This place is too quiet, he said. I need a buzz. Might go Stateside. Check out the scene there. He flicked away a magazine to the end of the sofa.

America?

You gonna come? Or do you like this chicken run of a city? He motioned to the towers beyond the window. Flower boxes on sills. Cramped rooftop gardens. A stranglehold of ivy on a trellis.

I can't up and go. It's too far away. And I'd have no job. I know I don't earn much at the college, but at least it's money coming in.

But this country's drab. And look at the weather. You could easily find a job. We could go skiing in Vermont. I've got friends there. And San Francisco, down by the water. Someone else I know has a house.

He stood blocking the light.

It's not so easy for me, I said.

Okay. Let's discuss it later. We can arrange something.

Talking for hours, they stayed up late while the rest of the city slept and kept company only with the fluorescent lights of empty office blocks.

He went to New York on business. He went again and came back. The third time he went, it was for good. He phoned once but didn't write. In the lengthening weeks of his absence everything between them was as wide as the Atlantic.

ARE YOU THERE? her father called from the bed. Is there a cup of water?

Catherine helped him onto the pillows. Feathery hair shimmered in the afternoon light. He drank before falling back asleep with his mouth open. She replaced three kinds of tablets in the back of his locker, ruffling up the lace doily under the vase of daffodils. The nurse would have done this, as her mother had done years ago.

He slept with breath coming easily, his face familiar, yet different. The skin on his throat sagged. Catherine made her way to the large window looking out over the beach, careful not to wake him.

At the edge of the waves, some boys were kicking a ball. Carson had liked football but rarely went to matches as he never had the time. Now it was probably baseball which captivated him. How successful had he become? It was either exceedingly or very. He would not have let any opportunities escape his grasp.

A woman was walking across the sand. Her headscarf fluttered in the wind. Catherine could have made use of this scene, this woman, if she'd had her pad to sketch in. How few sketches she had made of her mother.

Her father propped himself up on his elbows.

You're still there? he asked. What time is it? Have you a watch?

Ten to four. She sat down beside him.

The nurse'll be on with the tea. She makes me drink it, though it's terrible weak.

I've got to be going, Dad.

You'll be along tomorrow? Would you get me a little thing?

How little?

Some Players. His beady eyes glittered.

I certainly won't. If the nurse catches you, or I do...

It wasn't anything. Only a thought.

Well, you can forget it, Dad.

She bent down to kiss him on the forehead. The old devil, she thought. Trying to kill himself. Run out on me.

Before the nurse showed up, Catherine went downstairs. Her footsteps resounded like waves. She saw her mother standing on the rough part of the beach. A person could not hang on to anyone. Not in thoughts. Not in scents or sketches. She had to let go, or they'd go anyway. They'd evade. A brooch would be left behind. A paste pearl necklace. A sapphire ring might be passed down, or a few blues records, but nothing real. Nothing a person could carry or hold on to. *Washed away*, *washed away* echoed in the tone of her mother's voice in prayer, at one of her evening rosaries: an invocation to the beach, to all the beaches she'd ever known, from there all the way to Silhouette Island.

Crèvecœur

ALTHOUGH I HAD VISITED Madam Vernier and her husband Jean-Louis before, I couldn't see the N65. Golden cows munched in a field as flat and open as a book. I stopped at the rail crossing, though no trains ever ran and the station was derelict. Green paint flaked from the walls and flowers in pots on the sill had withered. *Mais, oui*, Madam had assured me. Trains do run. Towards the south.

I had never been south, to the wealth of fig trees and vineyards. But Jerome could not accompany me, as a training course had come up for geography teachers, so I was in Normandy on my own. Truthfully, I was relieved, for it would be easier to let the chill winds of loss blow through. The miscarriage had alarmed him more than me. I could manage the stumbling days ahead by myself.

I arrived at the farm with a longing for what was familiar. The Verniers presided over an immense acreage which surprised me the first time I saw it. I'd expected mud-spattered gates which never completely shut, small fields with hens running about. But the tractors were as tall as I was and the only animal the family kept was a pet rabbit. Madam gave me the best room. The view from my window overlooked the lush gardens, the orchard thick with shrubs and sprinkles of flowers, and, in the distance, through the mist, a chateau.

From the dining room downstairs, aromas of a sweet *bouquet garni* rose to entice me to supper. Fish or the chicken with apple? Madam and Jean-Louis lived on them, especially as he bottled cider, which arrived at the farm in huge vats. I would never cook like this, for all my kitchen skills evaded me and those I possessed had not impressed Jerome either. When I returned, I was sure he'd be less irritated with me than before I left. Even if he wasn't, it was good to take a break. I had lost my centre of gravity.

The large, dark wooden table was laid by Veronique, Madam's teenage daughter. The eldest of three children, she had long blonde hair and annoyingly spoke good English as well as German. She worked silently, attending to the ritual of the meal.

By eight, everyone had come in. First to arrive, after me, were the neat French man and his wife, who conversed only amongst themselves, followed by the couple from Barnes with two teenage boys. One of the boys had long hair flapping about his ears and, last night, it had dipped into his bowl of soup.

I had queried him about speaking French and the languages he was learning.

Are you a teacher? he said.

Yes, actually I am.

What of? he asked, perkily.

Art.

Beside him, his brother squirmed. I understood why. I didn't wish to be reminded of home or school either. I'd turned to the family of four from Derbyshire who'd driven here from the other side of the Alps. I pressed them for details on their journey, though the trip to catch the boat had been enough for me. Tom and his crowd sat nearby. The previous evening, when we'd sat together in the garden, he had referred to them as cotton tops. He'd explained how he was driving the eight, including an aunt and two cousins, to areas associated with French writers. Most of the group had never been outside America before, and none had been to Europe, but he had concocted this tour and they were enjoying it, I'd re-marked, if their chatter and laughter were anything to go by. They had been to Alençon, Chartres, and Rambouillet, visiting Norman and Gothic churches. All the wonders they'd been shown set them babbling with delight at the elegance and opulence of it all.

Oh *my*, said Yvonne to her neighbour. Did you ever see the statue in the church? The one with a garland on the head? Like a hat I got for my sister.

And you know, Maybelline added, the tiles in the hall we went to after lunch, I swear you could buy the same downtown. They do black and white, red, green, brown, and you can order other colours.

Do you know it wasn't even Mathilde's maidservants who made the tapestry? another lady chimed in. It was the priests. We even saw the place where Joan of Arc had her visions.

The women were full of praise for Tom. He was useful with his French, they said, and he had taught at the Sorbonne for the past three years. But if he hadn't confirmed this over coffee after the meal, when we sat up late together, I would never have believed it. He had the most Southern accent I'd ever heard and he exaggerated it in a way which made me laugh. Nothing about him matched with where he was. I could not work out what he was doing there at all, in France, but he said his family originated from New Orleans, and way back from the Languedoc, to which he hoped to introduce the group.

They're keen to go almost anyplace, he said.

They appreciate you. So what do you teach at the Sorbonne?

Basic English. To graduates.

You're going to stay in France?

If I can get a job. My girlfriend—well, she *was* my girlfriend. Not anymore. She was telling me about an opening in Lyon, but I'm rooted to Paris and the north. I love this country. Truly. Its history's got to me. I'm beginning to feel at home.

The next evening, he was at the far end of the table. Madam sat beside me and her daughter was quiet, so I had to work hard to make conversation with Madam and the couple from Barnes while trying to ignore their sons. The two adolescents were being obnoxious. They writhed in their seats and scrawled their facial features to draw a reaction from the girl. I had to fight the urge to call their behaviour to the attention of their parents. I wanted to say, Yes, it's true. Take it from me. I spend my days with teenagers. This is how they start and how they stay. Every awful thing you've heard is absolutely true.

Laughter came from where Tom sat. I wished I was in his company again. I could even have put up with hearing, for about the fourth time, how Roger, a park ranger from Missouri, had come across a rare snake and seen a naked jogger, or listening to Yvonne describe her days as a hairdresser and the various shades of black through to blue rinses. Everyone was talking at once. Jean-Louis had opened the cider and the Americans were on the wine. I drank because the cider was so rich and helped block out the presence of the boys.

After the meal, in the course of the evening, some of the others drifted away or upstairs to their rooms. Tom and I continued drinking. It was nearing midnight. He asked Jean-Louis for another bottle. He told me how, on Saint Patrick's Day in Chicago, it was possible to buy green Guinness, and he seemed ready to embark on a related story until I said I was sleepy and it was best I headed upstairs.

See you at breakfast, he called as I retreated to my room.

On Sunday morning, the Americans clattered through the dining room for breakfast while I lay in bed above. When I opened the curtains and looked out the window, beyond the fields and the orchard, the chateau reached for the sky like a pallid stone.

The Americans had already left, earlier than usual, for their long day of touring, when I went down. After breakfast, I drove out to the chateau, nearly missing it hidden behind trees. It stood tall and thin at the end of a long, gravelly driveway. I parked and made for the ticket booth, past the other visitors who all seemed to be pushing buggies, and I paid the price of entry. A path led to the main door where I stepped into a carpeted hall. I followed the carpet to a staircase and up to the bedrooms. Porcelain bedpans were displayed on cabinets. A little seat had been made for dogs. Chinese tables of dark lacquer showed trees with spillages of blossom on the ground. There were rosewood cradles, beeswax in chandeliers, blue glass and gold leafed Dresden. I could have drawn down the blinds, rung for coachmen or maids, dispatched servants and sent for notaries. I could have inhabited these spaces, lived within these rooms. A chest of drawers dripped with crisp white fabric, a Christening robe. A little cap balanced on a silver mug, with ribbons and lace spilling down shamelessly. I was tempted to touch the fabric and lose myself in the run of years which had been retained immaculately for the family of the house.

On the other side of a huge lawn, an obtrusive angular sculpture stood like a tree made of stone. As I approached, the branches came alive with a fire of rain. Had the owner seen me and set off a switch? At a wooden bridge over a pond, a model gondola sailed on the water and tones of Mozart came from hidden speakers. The machinations were clever, spellbinding.

TOM RETURNED TO THE HOUSE with his gang before me. The others had already made their way to the dining room, still some time before Madam would serve the meal, but I found Tom alone, in the sitting room, scrutinising a map. He looked up when I entered and his smile reached his eyes.

Hey, he said. How's it going?

Fine. And where did you go today?

Cabourg, Trouville, Deauville. Did they take to the hotel in Cabourg where Proust lived? Thought I'd never get them out. And do you know, it was empty. You'd think people would flock. But we had the lounge to ourselves and I got a peek at the dining room.

How did you manage that?

I walked in. It's right on the front overlooking the sea. All the gold and baroque. So great.

Do you think they'll read his work when they get back?

Tom shook his head.

They like the idea of him. They like his style, which is enough for them.

In the evening, Madam's exacting seating arrangements were more relaxed. The French couple had left and been replaced by an English-speaking family of four from Belgium. It was as if Madam had concluded since everyone could speak the same language, they may as well all get on with it. I made sure I was at Tom's end of the table this time. The other side was for recent arrivals, placed by Madam, I guessed, so they were nearer the door and the stairs, should they find the conversation too overwhelming.

Tom talked about Lisieux and the far reaches of Brittany. If I had not known him, the way he reeled off facts would have ann-oyed me. But, as it happens, I was beguiled, attentive to his tales and anecdotes, like the one about the Bishop of Bordeaux who had three children by the daughter of Charles II. Wine flowed and crumbs spilt over the table as everyone grew louder and more raucous.

By midnight, only Tom and I were left. His presence was a relief after a day of solitariness and the sense of bewilderment which stalked me when I thought of how, upon my return, I would have reports to write, exams to oversee, portfolios to send off. I shivered in a kind of pain at leaving the farm.

What's wrong? he asked.

Tomorrow, all this ends.

So, what was your last day like?

I went to the chateau.

There are lots around. Too many damn aristocrats. He laughed. You mean the chateau nearby? Due east?

I can see it from my window.

You know the story? The guy who built it came back from war and created it for his fiancée, who was Austrian. He had everything made *just so*, to make her feel at home, but she left him and went off with some other lord or duke. So: *Crèvecœur*.

Tom pronounced the word with a flourish. For me, the language always slipped out of my reach like an exotic bird.

What does that mean? I asked.

Broken heart.

The words bit, snuck up on me and dug in their teeth.

It was refurbished after the Second World War, he said. They used it as a hospital and pretty much wrecked it.

I delighted in drawing him out, making him feel he was directing a blind voyager through a world of abundance.

There are extraordinary gardens, I said. I expected it would be dull and predictable but I came out feeling uplifted.

Would you like to try a liqueur? he asked, leading me to his room. I mean your last drink? It's a kind of Calvados.

I sat on a hard-backed chair while he poured. I drank and pretended not to notice when he poured more. It was warm to my throat after the meal.

I bought it in a town yesterday when we stopped for lunch. What do you think? I'm not sure it's as good as the real thing.

The liqueur glowed as if a garnet was sunk at the bottom. Almost too good to drink, I thought, but I sipped anyway.

Yes, I said. The real thing.

Come, he said, setting his glass on a bedside table and taking mine.

I saw only his eyes as he led me down. He leaned in, hands struggling with my blouse and jeans. I closed my eyes. I did not mind. Let it happen. Let it come raining down. My body would not give me away. Gone and damaged. What had been done was done. I turned, not daring to find his face. *Crèvecœur*. It pulsed through every fibre in my body. I saw a glowing heart in my grandmother's house, in the picture of Christ above the mantelpiece. A torturous red. Did it really glow or did it take its glamour from the little light beneath it? My grandmother had married at eighteen. She had been a pretty young woman, sought after, who was generous to all who came to the house and kept a girl to help. And she had ten children.

My breath was short. Tears welled but I would not let them fall. I thought of the fat little figs at a local market which I had bought and gorged on.

Tom rolled off. I turned to find him on his side, but facing me, with tears of his own prickling the corners of his eyes.

What's wrong? I whispered.

I guess, he began, it's Sophie. I think I'm not... I haven't gotten over her. I thought I had, but I haven't.

I laid a gentle hand on his head. At my touch he closed his eyes.

It doesn't matter, I said and kissed his eyelids and in the faint light I saw his complete nakedness, like a child's.

The baby had been sucked out of me, lost to the void of the world. My body could not be a home.

Tom squeezed his eyes in a torment and rose from the bed, battling with his shirt tail to cover his naked bottom.

I'll be off in the morning. Probably before you're up. I padded over to him.

Do you have to?

I must. I can't miss the sailing.

Goodbye, he said, but he clutched my hands.

It's been lovely knowing you. I kissed his cheek and he let go my hands and the sudden quiet cut me as I retreated to my room.

IN THE MORNING, I pulled back the curtains. The chateau was barely visible in the new day's mist. A nothingness. Yet a presence. I tried to believe something was still out there. Was this not what I'd learnt in school on long afternoons of catechisms?

I drove out of the village, over a river to a neighbouring town. Tom's blue minibus stood in the square but he was nowhere to be seen. A cat walked along a wall. An old man entered a *boulangerie* and a woman came out with two loaves. It was eleven o'clock and quiet. Inside the large church, Tom would be intoning details about the stone and the windows, pointing out the features of marble sculptures and wooden carvings, telling his eager listeners about structure, masonry, solidity, survival through time.

I drove until I arrived at the wharf. In a cabin so sharp and metallic it could have been a hospital room, I lay on the lower bunk, but a piano tinkled and beguiling, lilting jazz seeped through the walls as we sailed. I could not sleep and went up on deck. The sea was tremulous and lurching. When I leant over the railings, a foaming undercurrent charged as the boat in the night was freed from the land. Though I might never see it again, the stones of the chateau would live on, as they had through wars and battles, sickness and hopefulness, its pale spirit ghosting from what it was to what it had become.

Grievous Bodily Harm

WE KEPT MEETING THE COUPLE from Bournemouth in the bar, every evening during Happy Hour.

Can we sit here? Cheryl whimpered.

Other hotel guests drifted in. There was the pair from Manchester whose voices echoed off the ceiling and the redhead with the tiny husband. There was the tall German boy and his two demure sisters; they had to be sisters because they both had a way of darting, birdlike, for the small pots of jam at breakfast. The others chatted. Ron was good with people. He knew the right subjects to talk about: rates, mortgages, property prices in England, prices in Portugal and Spain.

WE'RE GOING TO the far side of the beach tomorrow, Cheryl announced.

Where is it? Colin asked.

Over beyond the outcrop. It's said to be very beautiful. Only the locals know about it.

We should go there, too. Colin turned to me. The beach. What do you think?

We'll let you know what it's like, Cheryl said.

I put down my drink on the delicate paper coaster. The paper had the wings of a dragon emblazoned on it.

You don't look very enthusiastic, Colin said to me.

It would be nice to see more of the beach, I said.

Through the window, I saw, the water of the bay captured the smudgy shadows of a cliffside restaurant. Nearby, local boys were playing football and filling the darkening air with their cries. Raz had been, still was, their age, and had their exuberance.

HEY, MAN. You're not my social worker, Raz said in feigned surprise in the doorway to his flat. Snow packed the corridor. Only the lift up the block had offered relief from it.

I am. I flicked through the papers in my hands, attempting to adopt an officious tone. He had deep, wistful brown eyes.

You're too young.

Sorry, I shrugged. You're stuck with me. Is there somewhere we can sit?

He let me in. The living room had a long sofa against a bare grubby wall. His legs splayed open as he watched me, waiting for me to begin the speech which, according to what I'd read, he'd already heard twice before.

You're lucky not to have been given a custodial sentence, I said, but the judge took everything into account so it's important you keep your probation appointments—

Two weeks later, in my office, he rubbed his knee.

It's painful to stand, he said and set his foot on the floor.

Doesn't stop you coming to see me. You should've come last week. Failed appointments won't look good in the report.

No. I can do without.

He tipped back in his chair. I hoped he wouldn't hit the wall.

You can't do without it. Believe me. The magistrates will decide your future on it.

COLIN LEANT OVER the coffee table. I put away the brochure about tours in the mountains.

Did you hear? We'll go to that restaurant tomorrow. Lanterns, by the cliff. Meet Cheryl and Ron there? He said it was a good place for a fish meal.

At eleven, on the beach, a blonde girl settled in front of us in the company of a thin boy whose Rastafarian locks swung like braids of seaweed. The boy wore red and white board shorts and caught the attention of a Turkish family sitting on the sand nearby.

You from Germany? the bulky father called to him.

Frankfurt, the boy said.

My brother was there, three years. He like it. You work?

No. My girlfriend and I are students.

Ah, *studenta*. The man beamed and straggled to his feet. He crossed the sand and walked up close to the couple so I could only hear stray words like *factory, cinema, government*.

The boy's hair glistened. Raz had always kept his cut short, like a skullcap.

RAZ RUSHED INTO THE OFFICE, his backpack half off his shoulder.

I looked up. What's wrong?

The man at the door?

The porter?

He asked if I had an appointment.

All the time. You should have said. I laughed.

His eyes were like the dead glass in the cars round Brixton. I shivered with the raw knowledge I had hurt him.

Well, what have you been up to this week? I asked.

Working for my brother-in-law. Roofing.

Is it legal? No, never mind. I don't want to know. I hope you're insured. In case you fall or anything.

I know. No compensation. But it won't happen to me, man. Just write me a good report, yeah? I been keeping all these appointments with you. I'm hanging on.

ON THE BEACH, I turned the pages of *La Douleur*. The horizon was low and almost indistinct, a thin line between two slightly different shades of pale blue.

It's midday, Colin said. We've been out for more than two hours. You shouldn't stay any longer.

It's all right. I've got number twenty-five on.

Well, I'm going back. I don't want to get too exhausted for the meal tonight.

He strode off. He wore a sun hat, long trousers, and a long-sleeved shirt: the best-dressed Englishman on the beach. He passed the boy from Frankfurt, playing football with the Turk's three sons, and turned to watch the yellow and red ball glide across the sand.

Ah, *goala, goala!* the boy cried.

I felt young and energetic hearing the children. My skin baked. I was warm and pleasured. Eventually the boy sat on his towel with his girlfriend close and spread suntan oil on her back. The girl had full breasts. I dozed against the smatterings of German words. When I opened my eyes, the boy and his girlfriend were jumping the waves like flying fish. Up and down, holding hands. The girl laughed amid the fractures of the crashing swell.

THIS IS QUITE A GOOD REPORT you've got from college, I said, flipping through the pages on my desk.

It weren't a bad place. I can write better now. I'm glad you got me in.

There's another course we've got vacancies for. More advanced. You'd learn more than functional skills. Learn some special kind of work you could do afterwards. And there's one evening you've got to attend.

I passed Raz the glossy prospectus and he eyed the photographs of the students' common room, the canteen, the gleaming computer workshops. When he came to the final pages he lingered over a colourful shot of a disco.

One whole evening? he said.

What's wrong with that?

The seventeenth. I'm busy.

You need to learn something you can earn a living with.

Oh. Man. Too much.

Come on. I passed him the enrolment form, which I'd already filled out with his basic details. Sign this. It's a good bet on your future.

Raz scanned the prospectus and sighed. All right. He took the enrolment form from me. I guess it doesn't look too bad after all, he said. I slid a pen across the desk. As he picked it up, he said, You know what?

No. I thought back over the syllabus for the first term. It mentioned the emphasis on practical skills.

You—eh, you look a bit like my friend's sister. He signed the form.

Really? I said.

Yeah. He passed the pen back to me and laid the form on the desk. She plays good music and she can play the piano. Can you play?

No. I gave up lessons years ago.

You like music, though?

Everyone likes music, don't they?

What kind of music you like? Jazz, rock? Soul?

All three.

Want some vinyls? He leant forward in his chair, but without touching the desk. It wouldn't cost you.

I can't.

Out the window, workmen in high-vis jackets were digging up the street. In the overcrowded office, the grey metal filing cabinet needed replacing to hold the folders which had begun to spill over the floor.

Why not? Raz asked. What's wrong with some vinyls? You've not got the gear to play them? Don't worry. They're not nicked.

I'm not allowed, I said, plucking another paper from the pile on my desk. Let's get on with this breakdown of your week.

I saw him out of the office at four thirty. At the door, he stopped in front of me and ever so gently, as if taking a piece of guava or lychee, he put his lips on mine. I shrank from him in alarm, a confusion of need and outrage. The door swung back as he left. I checked his file, a history frozen in the landscape of a quarto: breaking and entering, driving in possession of an offensive weapon, handling stolen goods.

On Christmas Eve, I worked late. On my way out, the porter called.

Miss O'Meara. Package.

He pushed the brown parcel towards me.

My name was a childish scrawl. The fool. He'd end up costing me my job, just as I was applying for a senior grade.

Thanks.

I took the parcel home. It turned out to contain Nat King Cole's *Unforgettable* and a selection of Miles Davis. A week later, during a sluggish afternoon on duty, I received a call from the police to inform me Raz Deniston had been apprehended on suspicion of robbery and charged after resisting arrest. His New Year would be spent on remand, in prison.

My skin was hot by three o'clock on the beach. The couple nearby were gathering their things. The blonde girl folded towels and put them into a basket, including the towel the boy had been sitting on.

Goodbye, the Turkish man called to the boy. See you tomorrow?

No, said the girl. We return to Germany. This is our last night.

I am sad. But you have good time?

Ja, said the boy. Very good time. Goodbye.

The couple crossed the sand. The ends of the girl's shirt trailed after her. The braids of the boy's hair swung to and fro in tandem with his stumbles.

WHAT KIND OF A DAY did you have? Cheryl asked. We had to check each couple had managed to survive despite the distress of the other's absence.

She's got through a pile of books, Colin said. Haven't you?

What are we going to have to eat? asked Ron.

We peered at the menus. We hadn't made decisions by the time the waiter arrived, so we floated ideas aloud as he hovered by our table.

Lambs' brains? I suggested.

What? asked Colin.

You know I like to try different things.

Not *that* different. What about the main course?

I'll have a mussel kebab, Cheryl announced.

The same, Colin added.

A lamb kebab, please, I said.

The same, said Ron. And soups as well, for everyone.

The starters arrived. A saxophone seared the night air. I was cold but the music made up for not having a cardigan. I ate the chilli. It burned my mouth. I gasped for relief from the tingling, the flames inside.

Can I—I need some water, I said.

Colin summoned the waiter and had a bottle of water brought to the table. A tuba let slide a shock of notes. I drank.

Are you all right? Colin asked.

My stomach screwed up inside me. I couldn't breathe and I felt as if I might fall off my chair. Raz's face came to me in a flash, dark as the evening sky and the sea.

I'm sorry. It's nothing.

You sure?

It's nothing, I said, and kept on insisting, to the waiter who carried me up the path to the hotel room. Colin trailed behind us.

You been out today? the waiter asked. He helped Colin walk me to the bed and when I lay down I saw him gazing at my pink legs. You been out, he said. Is sunstroke.

You're burnt. Your legs, and your arms. Your stomach, too, I'm sure. Colin raised my dress a little, enough to see the scorching mound and show me.

I look awful, I said. But it didn't seem I was a long time on the beach.

You got to get yoghurt and put on all over, said the waiter. Let dry, and wash off. You do this a lot of times. It good.

My skin's hot, but I feel chilled. I started to shiver.

What have you done to yourself? Colin asked. I told you to come up with me. Where shall I get the yoghurt from?

Shop on the corner is open, the waiter said. Try there.

My teeth chattered uncontrollably. I had been hot but was cold, deep inside.

I'll be back, Colin said as he and the waiter moved to the door. They stepped outside together and the door swung shut behind them. Suddenly I was alone in the cool of the room, like the office at the Civic Centre, in the busy street where the tower blocks grazed the sky and traffic breathed fumes all day. Raz had come once, twice, in the depths of the cold and would not come again.

Dark Rain Falling

Now the sky was washed clean of clouds, light poured down as the rain had done on earlier days. Relentless radio reports had told of surrounding villages flooded, road closures, buses stuck, stranded. The two hundred-year-old bridge in Lettermore had been reduced to a crumble of grey stone.

Kaye followed the walkway, a Victorian pier from the hotel to the beach. It had been constructed for genteel ladies to take the air, according to the hotel brochure, and so she saw women with frilled bonnets and parasols strolling to the end, but not too far, retreating to the spread of trees nearer the gardens. Further out, past dunes where grasses snagged the wind, the pier was cracked. A fissure exposed a rub of orange rust on iron joints and clips; wood weathered and split, joists hewn apart, the bricolage of elemental damage. But staying at the hotel for the weekend was not so foolish, she told herself. The worst of the rain was over.

Along the strand a woman walked a dog. She wore a green beret, small protection against the weather, but still, thought Kaye, protection of a kind. At the edge of the sea, waves chucked themselves up in the last gasps of a storm. Kaye sat on a boulder by tricklets of pools. A couple of months back, children had played here, had run and squabbled, gathered sand, trawled for treasures to fill buckets, and she might have wandered down to the shore to sketch, but Gerard had become clingy and discouraged her. He had grown more dependent and although, on some level, this might have been what she wanted, his needs were also stifling. As they were fortunate enough to enjoy the freedom to be together, he'd said, she should not let her interest in art carry her away.

Tresses of seaweed writhed over the rocks. She raised a handful of dark knots and they dripped torn and pulled like a flurry of wild hair. Dried scabs of mussel shells had chipped like nails from their hard ridges. Lips of the sea. Purses of night. Blue intensifying to lavender at the base. A bruise of deep ink.

SHE HAD NOT NOTICED the bruising until sitting on the toilet at home. In the sandalwood aroma of the white tiled bathroom, she'd pulled up her dress and saw, on her gloopy thighs, a stain. Darkened capillaries milled into a desert of mauve. The smash and grab of her. And at her knee, scratches from his nails. In time, the marks would dull to the brown of dank leaves, waxy yellow, a smudge of peat, and gone.

THE COUPLE AHEAD were old country folk, she supposed, for he wore a cap and she a headscarf as they headed towards the church. Married, probably, as most people were. Although she knew this was fanciful and not the case. When she had started teaching at the girls' school, everyone seemed to be married. Her friends. The girls' parents. Or, if not, they at least belonged in couples. She had known he was married, at the start at the teachers' conference, because he had mentioned his wife and worn a ring. He had not deceived her. It was an inconvenience they'd managed to overcome with planning: small hotels, long weekends. She became good at working out routes and over the year they must have travelled to every county. The first time in a rented cottage near Youghal he had snaffled her, nibbling her stomach, rising to her breasts. The lip and lick of him drenching her with spit and semen as they had rolled in and out of all the places of each other. Longing had warmed her through for days afterwards.

A trail of lights necklaced the quay with odd ones missing, knocked out by the previous night's rain. A couple of trawlers at anchor, a speedboat, a *currach*. A self-important red yacht which could not have belonged to a local.

In the foyer, diners were visible beyond the smoky glass screen, lost to the clamour of eating, the jitter of cutlery and chitchat between couples with little of meaning to say.

Can I help? asked the boy at the desk.

Might I have a pot of tea brought to my room?

Of course. His raze of a beard was gingery and he smiled with ease, but he was pale as if he'd rarely been outside this side of the summer. He added, You're not too late for dinner.

It's all right, thanks. I'll have a sandwich too. Ham. Or anything but cheese.

Right you are.

In her room, sitting on the bed, she relished the taste of soda bread and the slink of salty butter such as her aunt had made. When she returned the tray to the front desk at gone nine, the boy was lugging a sandbag to the front door. He knelt to shift it into position, pulled another to stack on top.

More rain? she asked.

So says the fella on TV.

A long day for you?

It is. Some of the others couldn't get to work because of the roads.

He pulled out a sandbag from a pile and she bent to help him, to grip the other side, so they could shift it in one movement towards the door. The sandbag sank like a drunk and she kicked it into place.

You've a good hit, he said.

If you want a thing in place you have to make it secure. She smiled.

True. I don't want any bit of water in. We've enough already. The lawn in the bag is marshy and'll take some draining. He stepped back, wiping his brow. Thanks, he said. These are new fellas. We've some from last time, of course, but you can never have too many.

AS SHE LEFT FOR BREAKFAST, he was pushing a trolley along the corridor. He slipped into one room, leaving its door open, and set about making a bed, snipping in the corners of the sheets. The trolley was piled with linen and towels in the lower section, with packets of biscuits and tubs of milk on top. She swiped a fresh towel and sunk her face into its brilliant pile. She let the fresh aroma seep into her and before she set off she took two packets of bourbons.

No-one else was up except for two suited men at separate tables. Business or funeral, she guessed. At the buffet she ladled blueberries and raspberries into a large bowl and took two glasses of juice to revive herself. Before she had urged him to leave his wife, she'd drunk two shots of whiskey. Then she issued an ultimatum. After these months, she'd told him, we owe it to ourselves: her or me. She had not thought her words would sound so strong or deliberate, yet they'd come out rising in a demand: We can't go on. Two years like this, buzzing between hotels. Avoiding towns where we might run into someone one of us knows. Two years is enough. Be fair to her. And to me.

He'd kept his elbows on the table, held his face in his hands.

HE CAME UP WITH REASONS, as he had before when they skirted the subject. Too soon. Too much for his wife to bear. He needed more time. She had let his reasoning stand, saddened by his dilemma. His eyes were dark with worry and afterwards, as she drove back alone, she chided herself for being precipitous. What was the point of burdening him with stress? They had each other. They had each other in ways she liked and which were convenient, most of the time. He was always at the end of the phone, if not always there for her in person, and he showed up in real life whenever he could manage it. Showed up at his best, not worn out by a trudge through days of domesticity; showed up with effort, for her. She bit her lip for in many ways it was convenient indeed.

When they next met, he was at a seminar for deputy principals in Dublin.

You must say something, she said.

I will. Of course. I want you. He grasped her hand in the French restaurant off St. Stephen's Green. I want us to be together, he said. He traced a finger around her face and over her mouth and across her cheek, to her ears, where the gold of his ring hit. He said, I want all of you.

AT THE FRONT DESK, the boy was on the phone. He spoke in a raised voice and kept his back to Kaye as he huddled in a corner. A girlfriend, she thought. She could never make calls at work or receive them. Not unless she took refuge with her mobile in a spare classroom. But he had never called her. Texts only, they'd agreed.

The boy put down the phone.

Sorry about that. My mother...

Is she okay? After the floods, I mean?

She's okay. But she gets anxious. Panic attacks the last couple of years.

Kaye was touched at his telling.

Since my dad left, he said. She phones every day.

I suppose mothers always worry.

I guess so. You going for a walk? The pier'll need repair or there'll be accidents but heaven knows when the council'll do it.

She went out anyway. For space. For light. The beaches she had visited with him raced through her mind. Beaches in France and Spain. They'd visited the Île de Ré and he had remarked upon the women in elaborate white headdresses, a custom sustained, he said, because it was an island, as the isles of Aran kept their traditions. He said they'd catch a boat from Galway to Inishmore in the spring.

Walking in the opposite direction to the previous day, Kaye found the bay opening out and becoming wilder, free of buildings, with scrabbles of rocks and shingles and the stray tangles of seaweed. She carried the necklace in her pocket. Here was a good place to have done with it. Pointless to keep such a gift, for she would not wear it even though she had loved peridot and tourmaline. He'd bought it for her when they were in Nice. An impulsive flurry of a weekend arranged at the last minute when his wife was away with her sisters. He'd taken Kaye's arm along the Promenade des Anglais and found a jeweller.

No-one else will remember this, he said. He stood behind her and draped the necklace around her to fasten it. When he kissed her nape, his words lodged in her heart.

And now? Better off in the sea than bothering her, or beckoning her, at the bottom of a drawer every time she searched for clean underwear. Taken and carried away on the tide. Only a means to win her, keep her against the odds. And yet. Her fingers wrapped around the chain and the cuts of stones. Was it not a waste to throw it to the waves?

WHEN HE ANNOUNCED he had told his wife at last, she'd been caught unawares and realised she hadn't believed he'd ever be so bold. They had sat in a bar in a hotel in Longford while the business of the town swelled outside and traffic passed through, to and from Dublin. His face was ashen as he relayed his confession. His wife had called him brutal, cruel, a man of low morals, entirely selfish. He had agreed and she had stormed off, slamming the door behind her. Later, when his wife had recomposed herself, she told him to find somewhere else to live and hurled more stony words at him. The more he relayed, calmly, quietly, the more Kaye could hear the firestorm devouring their domesticity.

He had found a flat above a hairdresser and went back and forth between there and his old home to gather his possessions: vinyl records, suits and shoes. But afterwards he drew deeper into himself, grew quiet, sullen. Once, when they had stayed in a country house in the Burren, he found he had forgotten to bring his favourite jacket and so he mooned around for hours, depleted, lost for the lack of it. It seemed to Kaye as if a whole part of his life had gone the same way and she could not lift him out of the lows. He'd had to leave behind other favourites, a chair and Edwardian desk with a run of little drawers up each side, and she sensed he blamed her for it. But he'd been the one to suggest the weekend in Belfast. They might be together more easily, he'd said, knowing no-one there. Plus they could visit the Opera House and the new concert hall near the docks. A possibility of his coming back to life had flickered before her.

They returned to their room from a meal in the hotel restaurant where he enjoyed two bottles of red wine with his lamb casserole. He lay on the bed. The lone flare of a rose stemmed from a slim vase. Accommodating the pillow behind his head, he stretched an arm towards her. She hovered by the bed and said she could not go on. Wanted to break things off. Cold anger filled his eyes. He lunged. Grabbed her. Pinned her on the grisly pink candlewick bedspread. His fingers. His grip at her neck. In the small of her throat. Her voice like a trapped bird. His, full of gravel. You bitch. All I've done. The things I've given up for you. His thumbs pressed into her, hard, as his whole body thrummed with rage. She forced his head away from her, caught the skin of his cheek on her nail, and tried to prise him off her until he relented, deadened with either the effort or the fill of drink, and fell back onto the bed. In the bathroom, she gathered a few toiletries and smoothed out her clothes. She picked up her handbag and left.

THE NECKLACE DANGLED off the edge of the dressing table. Faint light caught on the chips of its stones as Kaye pulled the door closed.

Downstairs, the boy at the front desk was checking a computer screen while other guests breakfasted on black pudding and wilting bacon.

Hello there, he said. Did you hear the rain in the night?

I did not.

A blast from the sky. I thought the window frames in the old part of the hotel'd be blown out. There won't be many people about today.

She paid the bill and stepped outside. Light green moss dressed the trees. Distant fields floated in a mist as she left, as she drove away. The chain, the stones, released at last. The boy's mother might make good use of the piece. Might be charmed and drawn to wear it. When he cleaned the room, he'd find it. Driftwood brought to his shore. The sea, unruly, agitated, depositing debris before its retreat.

Araiyakushimae

THE SWAMP OF TEA BAGS near the sink grew with each one she threw on. Almost the end of her trip home and she'd dropped scraps of meat and packaging into the same bin for two weeks. Either the council's refuse collectors didn't care or her mother didn't, but pale chicken skin slid against tins and plastic containers which once held tomatoes. She wanted to delve into the slush, remove each item and divide the lot as she had done in Japan: a separate container for refuse to burn, food, and everything else.

You ready, Yolande? her mother called. Let's go while the day's still good.

The sun glimmered on the lake as they drove west. The lingering warmth was unusual at this time of year. Everywhere people claimed she had brought the fine weather with her. She hoped so, hoped landscape might be medicinal for her mother. Anyone undergoing tests deserved it.

The shortcut took them through the bog, lumpy rustland with a hush of heather. Mustardy tones she hadn't seen for years. Out on the main road, leaves glowed like embers in fires. Studs of orange berries in the trees, strands of tiger lilies running wild. Soft pink briar roses. She realised hadn't been around to see these things since leaving for college. She'd gone this way with Mickey when she had started at the secondary school and he'd offered to drive her to the bus in town. They'd taken a ride in his van, windows steaming, as the days shrugged away from summer. Ropes swished

47

in the back and his toolboxes rolled around. She'd rubbed at the vapour to make a hole to see out.

By the pier, with the Cloughmore mountains sliding against the sky, Yolande stopped and leaned over to release her mother's door. A light breeze caught it as it swung open. Her mother sat in profile against a cliff edge, her pale skin drained of blush and her cheeks having lost their roundness. But her eyes were the same sharp blue as always and she wore lipstick in case she met a neighbour or someone important: the doctor, the priest.

Revives a person, doesn't it dear? Getting out. Her mother's hands lay clasped in her lap like a closed purse. And you've been lucky with the weather.

Her mother, once strong, had been able to walk for miles over rocky paths and hills. But in the past month, since treatment began, Yolande had come to see her mother's internal systems churning with medications and radiation, crumbling inside. The things hospitals do to you, her mother had said.

They sat on a bench, an orange scarf concealing her mother's throat. How many more drives might there be before Yolande would have to return? With the span of oceans between continents, there was little she could do, but while she was still around she'd drive her mother anywhere she wanted to go.

Far out, the sheer cliff nipped into the sea. Clefts and eaves of rock, ridged with gorse and heather. Seabirds scrapped, their squalls rising. Waves broke in flips, charged at the coast in steady rolls. Far out, surfers rode the swell and slipped over the surface like tiny fish. Matsuko had told her he had walked in the alps north of Tokyo. When she'd asked him about sea cliffs in Japan, he'd laughed and told her most of the coast was too unstable for footfall. Instead they had lounged over long weekends in cities and smaller towns inland. He had introduced her to Onsen, his favourite, a traditional one by the sea, and she had sat on a boulder by a warm pool as steam rose from the mineral water and the women were glazed with light and she had supposed the same was happening to him, in his section.

We'll call on Mickey, her mother said. You should see him before you return and he might be in. She gestured towards the garden road whose little houses stretched beside long fields.

Would you like to? Yolande asked.

Oh yes. He's been low. He'll be glad to see us.

How d'you mean?

The poor fella's not been right for months. Down in himself.

Unsure what her mother meant, they returned to the car and Yolande drove on. Mickey hadn't been mentioned in phone calls or emails. A reedy man, her father's younger brother, he was the only one besides her parents who hadn't joined the others off to England or America.

She had wondered, while at school, did Mickey not know? Could he not see she wore a dress and not her old jeans? She had thought his brushing fingers on her thigh were a kind of mistake, how as an uncle he hadn't realised. Until again. When he came to visit on a Sunday afternoon. Her parents were in town. His hand rising. The nub of his thumb at her knicker edge, until she shifted off the chair at his table and stepped away. The third occasion, at the back of his house, he was eager to devour her and caught her shoulder, pulled her so she had to kneel. She'd told no-one. Let it choke.

The way he is, no woman'd put up with him, her mother said. Smoking and reading the papers till all hours. Only ever going to market and town.

He'd been bright. At school until he was sixteen. He should have known. Must have known. She stopped the car at his house, reluctant to go inside. In Japan, she had been shy to enter shrines and temples, fearful of stepping into a sacred space. On the new continent, she had tried to put the past behind her and for the most part, in the tight streets of Tokyo, in the rush of catching trains to work, in the work itself, she had managed to do it. The very tautness of daily life had freed her.

Mickey ranged the kitchen, tall, unsettled, searching cupboards. He didn't raise his head to acknowledge them.

Hello. Her mother greeted him while he opened one cupboard, then another.

I've no minestrone, he said.

Come here and talk to us.

I won't. He bent to a low cupboard, opened it, and scanned the shelves.

We were passing.

Ah, passing. Passing.

Yolande drove us.

Yolande, he repeated as if naming a brand of soup.

His eyes, when he stood, were russet dark, and his face had drawn thinner. He seemed taller than Yolande recalled and it took her a moment to realise it was because he'd lost weight. Most likely due to working in the fields, cutting rushes or making silage. His movements were twisty with nerves and he would not sit.

How are you, Mickey? Her mother continued.

Hungry. For there's the sheep to ready for the show. He opened a tin and poured its contents into a pot. He set the soup to warm on the gas. They let him sit and eat, and drink, though he made no offer of tea. Finally he pushed away his empty bowl. I've to get on, he said abruptly. Have to be there by three or what'll the other fellas think.

He had not noticed her. She may as well have been a sack of potatoes. They followed him out and he opened the gate to the field, tying it to the post with blue plastic string. She should say something. Speak. After so long she must. She wasn't the confused girl who had feared upsetting her parents. The notion pounded. Reverberant like a hammer dropped in a box. She should make him see the small damage. Before he got older and it was too late. Let him know of the humiliation which had lain with her, trembling and churning, so it was not until she left college she had a proper boyfriend. Even then a sliver of fear. A trace. Until Japan, continents away, where Matsuko's gentle manners charmed her.

Mickey pulled a sheep from the pen, grabbing its head with a twist. It scampered with shock, the sticks of its black legs skittering in a kind of dance as though it did not know its own weight. Astride the animal, he held the face up and back with a deft flick of his wrist until the sheep calmed and he drew it to the small trailer. He slung it into the cab so it knocked against the tin.

Delaney won last year and I want to beat him.

Mickey rubbed his hands together and surveyed the sheep.

Of course, her mother said, though despite his years of entering he'd never won a thing.

No more than the Texel's or Suffolk. You can't beat a black face mountain one. He ran his hands across the back of the sheep and underneath, over the teats. He pulled open the mouth.

Teeth held all, Yolande remembered from when Mickey had bred horses. But sheep, he'd said, had only one set of teeth, so it was vital they met the upper gum in alignment. He hugged and twisted the head and even from a distance she could see the animal's blue eyes grow shivery with light. He knew the tricks and turns of the livestock and she wondered which categories he'd entered. Yearling or Ram. Open. Restricted. In late August, he'd used to sit at his kitchen table with the floral plastic cloth and a stubby notebook, mulling it over.

You know them well and how to work with them, her mother said. Though a pharmacist's daughter, she had picked up the ways of the land. We won't delay you.

Yolande stood near the window, looking onto the field. She should ask. Why had he taken advantage. Betrayed her parent's trust. And hers. He was not the son of a poor farmer who might have been cabined with all his family, but of one who was prosperous. Had he not known better? It was wrong. All wrong.

Pull up some carrots for yourselves before you leave. Plenty of them. You can bring the rest back to the house.

You had good crops this year? her mother said, and in a lower tone, added, Whatever else, he can stir growth out of the earth.

Okay, Yolande said, I'll get them. She picked up a small garden fork from the outside sill where it had warmed in the sun.

She would return. When the sheep show was over and he had no distractions. He would have to listen as she spat out words caged in for years. She would challenge. Scald him with the truth.

At the lower field, the brambles were pimply and underdeveloped because of the early summer rain. The bridge over the ditch was an old door with a few split planks supporting it, though its appearance belied its strength for it had been there through all the years from the time when her grandparents were still alive. Old rainwater sumped the soil around it. Grass and reeds clotted the flow, shimmering gold under the full light of the sky. She had jumped over the ditch as a kid, lost to danger, rather relishing it and not realising ditches developed from runnels and brooks, following the contours of the land. An irrigation, necessary, without which neither her father nor anyone around might have raised their stock. A moisture so present, so plentiful. Part of the air she breathed. Part of what she'd longed for when she'd gone away.

One Sunday morning, after days in the Tokyo heat, she had taken a train into the mountains. During the week the office air conditioning clothed her in coolness, but at weekends the heat left her drained. By mid-afternoon most days, setting out into the city to pick up this or that item, her clothes would be moist with sweat and she'd be done for the rest of the day. Even the dainty hats the Japanese women wore, one of which she'd bought, did not shield her from the sun. The most welcome part of her day had become the bath she'd take when she returned home.

Along the railway line, miles of flats gave way to houses as the train left the city. The houses, modest at first, became larger and larger and broken up, spaced apart, by farmland and fields. As the train gained elevation, the fields became greener and were given over, unexpectedly, to plentiful rows of vines. She disembarked at midday, stepping into sunlight so intense it slammed the top of her head despite the baseball cap she wore. But the decreased density of buildings and people made it easier to bear, and at her leisure she wandered the town, followed the main street to the outskirts. At the far reaches, a path led under trees whose canopy was cooling. On a slim wooden sign were symbols and, beneath them, a word: Araiyakushimae.

The shrine at the back of the courtyard was smaller than others she'd seen, but with its red trimmed roof and gold filigree running like lace along the side, it had a gracious quiet about it. In the cool of the temple, one man sat in prayer while others straggled at the back. Yolande wondered if she might not join them and she thought of home. School. How she had been taught prayer was the essence of distilled thought.

She tripped down the steps to collect her shoes. Evergreen trees in the courtyard twisted around each other like people writhing, contorting, trying to get rid of themselves. At the other end of the courtyard, under a canopy, rose a greystone statue of a human figure, no higher than a child. At its feet a man, crouching, ladled water from a spring and poured it over the statue's head. He wore a grey backpack with a floppy, creased sunhat, and he smiled as Yolande approached.

Hello. I am Matsuko. Of the Language Association Guide Service. His lapel badge confirmed this with a logo like a bunch of grapes. I can give you tour of the shrine? Or the castle?

No. No, thank you. I can't stay long.

Ah. It's pity. He went on ladling, water gushing and falling. The statue was somewhat like a Buddha, but also somehow feminine. A wife, she thought, or an acolyte.

Araiyakushimae, she said. What does it mean?

It mean new waters of life. And we need this in the heat. He leant towards the statue and rubbed its head. If I rub—he pointed to the head and waist—and I ill, it make me better. I have bad eyes. Cataract coming. He removed his glasses and blinked, smiling into what he could not see.

Am I allowed?

Oh yes. You try. He handed over another wooden ladle, as long as her arm, and she dipped it into the trough. Drops rained down the figure.

KNEELING ON THE DAMP GRASS, she dug into the soil, pulling up carrots with the garden fork. She knelt as she had with Mickey's knees in her face at the back of the house, as he undid his trousers until she'd flown up, brushing against his leg, and run.

Florets of light green leaves strayed open as she wrenched and tugged. Soil caked her fingers, ridged her nails, clogged underneath them. The carrots, good sturdy bodies, lay on the ground, an odd glove of seven fingers. She gouged the largest. Scored and struck. Bashed in the lovely flesh. Made weals and gashes. The next and next, until seven were wasted with nice, clean cuts and lay like fallen soldiers, all the goodness out of them.

Her mother was sitting outside the house on a rickety dining chair as Yolande came up the fields. Mickey trudged to the back door. Carrying a plastic sack which once held feed or meal, he'd been down to the stack of turf. Stooped low, as if wizened, he set down the turf from his arms the way he might see a poorly child to rest. He shook his hands in release of the burden, turned and tugged the sack, with a scrape, as he loped along the concrete path.

They drove back in a kind of silence broken by passing reflections from her mother, thoughts on improvements to the road and the growing number of houses. With the views, one could build holiday homes which would repay the cost, and to which anyone from Dublin and Limerick, she was sure, would be eager to come. She leant forward to switch on the radio, unleashing a rush of outdated pop music. The local station still did not invest. No wonder everyone left for more exciting places.

A shame about the carrots. Usually he has beautiful ones. And sweet, too.

No. They weren't good. The wheel passed through Yolande's fingers.

A poor harvest, after all. One wouldn't know what had got to them. A rabbit. A fox.

In the evening, readying to eat at the local hotel, she showered in the bathroom downstairs, kept for visitors. Her father had built the extension years before with the help of Mickey, who even then, as far as she could see, mostly set breeze blocks in place. She would not go back to him. Time with her mother was more pressing. She had grown beyond this place, where the old were shrinking before her eyes. She stood in pools of water under the shower head, slathering creamy water around her shoulders, drops trickling down her breasts, onto her belly, over her thighs, down her legs. The warmth was soothing on her skin. She flannelled down the bruises of encounters, of words and glances, and carefully washed away the hold of the years.

Foraged Things

LIKE A FRAIL CURTAIN, or the skin of her father's hand impressed by bones, the wisp of leaf lay on the sill. Beside it, a stray branch: scaly, silvery bark. A chestnut leaf with a dried cluster of flowers her father had said were like flame tips. If she brought the outside in, she might recreate the times they'd shared and catch him.

She drew down the blind to the sill and concealed what she'd collected. Easier than explaining. Not that her mum would have noticed. She was weathering her own craziness, spending days shopping, running through rails of dresses and blouses, buying skirts she'd never wear but only return, saying they were too shapeless or expensive after all. Lia had gone with her the first time, following as her mother dashed distractedly from one shop to another, leaving naked hangers in her wake. Dresses were too short or too long. With too large a print or too small.

Walking away from the estate, she took the road to the lane and the path to where the trees began. Light firs. Her father had said they were planted only recently. As she walked on, down an avenue lined with lime trees, the trunks grew thicker, more solid. Under the trees, in a sort of arbour, she scooped away mulch and lay down on her jacket. Flights of leaves. Leaves like tiny lanterns. Dripful of lemony light. Trippy. The whole day pulled in. High branches scratched the sky. And always the skittering of birds, though she could not see them and wouldn't have known which types they were, apart from the usual: thrushes and robins and pigeons eating the food she'd thrown out to entice the others to

show themselves. Their songs filled her ears, made her feel alive.
Not numb with waiting for calls from her father. His news of going
to live in Canada. Here, once, he had pointed out the trails of rab-
bits, where voles hid, the setts of badgers. If she listened hard she
could hear a flutter of wings. Like someone escaping through the
trees. No other sounds but the breaths of branches. A sigh as they
shifted, settled.

The last time she and her parents had gone camping had been
for a week at the base of a mountain in the north. Her parents'
red and black tent had been like an alien capsule landing on the
coast of anywhere and she had lain in the dark, awake all night,
alert to the roar of the silence around her. Beneath her she felt
the press of cold earth. Overhead, a skin of nylon.

She wanted to sink down, right down, seep into the soil. Be
covered. Wasn't this what burial was like? And hadn't the Vikings
believed you should take things with you? She closed her eyes and
let all the calls of the forest flood in. Rippling song. Hush of leaves.
The bloody red of her eyelids drawn down. Until a scamper. Footsteps. She blinked open. The trees were still there, scaled upward,
and clusters of leaves, one on another and another. Fir cones, dry
and spiky, and pads of glowing green moss, soft as velvet. A dog,
smooth haired with perky ears, snooped, nosed the leaves, as a
man, tall, thin, held it on a string lead. He was tanned. Out of doors
a long time, she thought. Lia rose and the scrape of her boots
against the dry earth caught him. His eyes were deep brown, and
he had the smoke of a beard unkempt.

Madlenka! he cried. Here! The dog snouted the base of the
trees, inching along over the musky leaves. She's harmless, he said.
Don't take any notice.

The dog sniffed Lia's feet, found her out, and the man followed
the strain of the string. He pulled, jerking the dog's head, and
drew her to his side. Good girl. He patted his thigh.

The man sat on the ground against the base of a broad trunk and dusted down his jacket. He lit up, a spark flaring against the depths of the lower branches and a skirt of bushes running wild. He slipped the pack into his pocket. No-one she knew smoked anymore, apart from a couple of her friends and her mother, who had started up again and left packs lying around the kitchen and her bedroom. When Lia mentioned the risks they'd learnt about in school, her mother had become tearful and said, I wouldn't if I didn't have to. She'd stubbed out in a saucer. Always something to worry about. If not you, it's him. Cut from the same cloth, the two of you always going off.

Lia had skidded out the door. Slammed it shut behind her. Shut on the tides of regret her mother washed up nightly. But Lia would have none of it. No wonder, she thought sometimes. He's seeking a new life.

THE MAN WAS WITHIN THE TREES by a dirt track. She's better behaved than my last one, he said. He threw a stick, and another quick after, so the dog ran and jumped and twirled back on itself in excitement at what it had heard but could not see.

Oh, don't, Lia said. But what did she know about dogs? She should shut up. She'd never had a pet. Too much fuss, her mother had said, though her father had been okay with the idea. She'd won a goldfish once but this didn't count as a pet. It died, its tiny body floating in the fishbowl one morning, belly-up, until her father buried it.

The man pulled the dog close and released the string so she wore only a thin collar with studs. He patted the dog's sides and threw another stick.

Go on. Fetch.

What's her name?

Madlenka. Swedish. I worked there once. But she's better than my last. More obedient. The old fella got run over and I missed him till I got her.

The dog returned, nuzzling the man. He stroked her.

Where you from? he asked. Round here?

Not far off.

Neat little town. His fingers scoured a grassy patch. Though I ain't seen this fella before.

What is it?

Tawny mushroom. He peeled the skin off the top and slipped it into his mouth.

Aren't they poisonous?

Some, but not this. *Amanita fulva.* He pulled pieces off the cap of the mushroom and ate them.

That foreign?

Latin.

He rose and followed the dog who poked at the base of a tree. The dog yapped and made for the slope of ground towards the pond, rushed into the water with a splash.

I gathered a load of nettles once, he said. Dumped them in a pot for soup. And elderflowers one summer for a drink. Ah, what's this? He wiped a piece of pottery with his finger. Nice bit of an old tile.

She had once found a piece of pottery, a fragment of chalky red clay, but she'd thrown it away without a second thought. Something about its brokenness or it being hard to the touch. Real. Too real. Her mother had smashed plates against the wall when her dad said he was leaving. Her mother had been drinking upstairs and came down laughing, which became crying. It took two weeks to scrape the mess off the walls, make it look as if nothing had happened.

Lia bent to collect the empty husks of some nuts, minute cups of pale green which fitted her little finger.

Bye, she said, and walked off with a pocketful of stuff.

ON HER SILL SHE LAY THE LEAVES. They were like lace, darkly stained. She pushed aside the stones to make room. Her favourite was split open, a rage of pink which her dad had said was rose quartz. They'd found some in Scotland where they'd camped by a lake under big skies. He had lit the stove in the morning, balancing it securely with a round of pebbles, and brewed grainy coffee which made her spit. It had rained for days until a brilliant sun came out and lifted her mother's mood.

THE MAN WASN'T IN THE WOODS the next time and she felt the tug of an unexpected disappointment. Saturday afternoon. No sign. Everyone's free to do as they please, she told herself. She gave up hoping to see him, though she couldn't work out why it mattered. He was no-one. But he reappeared two Wednesdays later, as sweat laced the back of her neck and shoulders. She heard the dog on its lead, skittering along the path, and turned to find him rising up the slope of land from the pond. He stopped to unleash the dog and looked up into the branches. She followed his line of vision, thought how the branches rising were like the roof of a great church, or the arms of the woods locking the two of them in. Safe. Secure. Bound together in leaves with each leaf subtly different, sparkling with its own light. The dog ran towards her and sniffed.

Hello, the man said.

She smiled.

I'm too late. These are over. He held out a handful of limp bluebells. I shouldn't really.

Why not?

Kind of a protected species. But I couldn't help it. Anyway, more'll be up next year.

He sat on the scuffed earth, knees drawn into his chest, the dog running around him until he reached out and patted her down and she lay at his feet with her tongue dangling. He said, We walked up from Newtown.

Not too far.

It is when you're my age. He leaned back, stretched his legs and closed his eyes. He inhaled the fragrance of the wildflowers beside him. Ah, this is the place.

She sank to the ground at the base of a tree a little way off. Not close. Far enough to keep a distance. Let him know she wasn't stupid. She'd have him sussed. Her fingers fell upon a clutch of ferns, and she thought how she might pull up some and take them home as a background for the stones and leaves.

He leant forward, running his hands over the ground as the dog scampered off.

Cobnut. He peeled the floral outer leaf to reveal the nest of brown. Want some? When she shook her head he shrugged, tipping a handful into his mouth. Can't say they're full ripe, but anyway. He chewed and wiped his hand with his cuff.

Her dad had fried an egg on a pan on the camping stove, could tip it out in a flash with a flick of his wrist and straight onto a slice of bread. He had constructed a little stand from sticks to roast sausages, to boil an egg in an old tin. They had crouched to crack open the shells, the little nests of warmth passing between her hands. He'd camp when he got to Canada, he said. He'd live in Montreal but make sure he got out of the city and she saw him lost to plains and wide expanses, drawn away and never coming back.

The man rose to his feet before she had a chance to ask. He couldn't be living in the woods unless it was in the burnt-out blue car, up on its side near Power's Ground. A cage of melted plastic and blackened metal, of chrome streaked with dust, it would give shelter of a kind, even if the doors had been pulled off and the inside was smeared with petrol.

You're looking at me strange, he said.

You a soldier?

No. He laughed. No, not one of those poor buggers. Iraq? No. Why d'you think so?

Thought you looked like one. Like you've been in wars.

I have. Me own kind with women and other people. He gave another laugh, a croak. I travelled, but never went to those hot places. He bent and grabbed a spray of daisies, plucked them to chew their stems. As he chewed, the ends of the flowers stuck out of his mouth.

He walked to the open ground, clear of trees, by the pond. Midges, thick and heavy, hung above the water. She was drawn by the press of heat and the stillness, and followed him to the side of the pond. Her reflection in the dank green water seemed so solid she might lift it out and place it somewhere else. Madlenka approached and sniffed at grasses. Windblown seeds stuck to her coat and she spun around in irritation, trying to free herself from them. The man laughed and the dog came to him. As he drew her in, wrapping an arm around her, she perked her ears and wagged her tail. He scanned the dry earth to find a pebble, and threw it into the pond. Lia's reflection shivered in widening circlets of waves, globules of flickering light. It trembled as the dog rushed in, savaging the water with splashes.

Always after something, that one.

Madlenka rushed out, squelchy, shaking waterdrops off her coat, wetting everywhere. Lia brushed off the water, patted down the front of her jeans and T-shirt to dry out the darkening patches.

The man pulled at a bush, where holly wound around a sapling before making an escape towards a bramble, and picked at a flower, fruit or something.

Rosehip. He opened his hand to reveal the pinkish pods, like beads. He cut down the middle of one with his nail and popped the fruit into his mouth. He moved along the bush to pull off more.

Good for your health. My grandmother made syrup from them when we were young. He split another pod and ate it.

She hadn't thought of him with a grandmother, or a mother, or anyone. But if she wasn't joining him eating rosehips, she'd no point in being there. Whatever time it was, she should get back, even if her mother was not home.

SHE COULDN'T GO TO THE WOODS the next two days or at the weekend, but on the Monday she hurried. Her pace quickened as the trees came into view and roofs and warehouses fell away with their dots of satellite dishes shrinking into the distance until all she knew was the quiet.

She lay down at the foot of the oak, so old, older than houses, or cars or the road. The in-between scraps of sky were blazing blue and the tops of silver birches swayed. Glittering leaves. Never still. The soil was soft, easy to spread out on. Nobody knew. No-one came up that way. Unless. And she thought of how only she and the man were aware of the place and its riches and how they might be concealed, away from the roads and the world. He might come with the pad of paws and the snout of the dog at the ground. She found a bush with blue berries and white flowers and wanted to ask him what it was. She lay under the branches, it seemed for hours, but she knew it was not, and she understood he would not come.

THE NEXT FEW TIMES she went to the woods she didn't see him, nor on the days after. She must have said something to offend or put him off. Or he was ill. Or dead. He did not come any other day and the woods were hers and he had been a vagrant passing through.

THE WEATHER TURNED INSIDE OUT, to autumn. Her father was due to collect her from college but didn't show up. She stood at the corner of the street by the café and tried to ring him but he didn't answer until the evening. He gave her a pale excuse. He'd been caught in traffic the other side of town. Too tired to be angry or question him, she let him ramble on. There'd be visits, of course. He and the girlfriend would get an apartment big enough for her to stay in, with her own room. No sleeping on sofas or kicking anyone out of their bed. He laughed.

Yes, Dad, all right. See you. Though she was losing heart, her fears spiralling as he continued, he would pick her up the following week, the last before he left.

He would not change his mind. He was going to Canada. Travelling so far off. She drew up the blind and a splinter of wood fell from the sill, a coil of silvered bark. Also a leaf whose veins spanned like a fan. But too many pieces had piled up. She should get a box. Wasn't this what people did? Pile them in and out of sight. Tidy her room.

HER MOTHER STOPPED SHOPPING WEEKLY, preferring, she said, to pick up things as they needed. Her mother had given up eating almost everything, existing solely on biscuits and crisps. The fridge held only a slab of hard cheese, two slices of dried ham, and a half-eaten peach yoghurt. No instant coffee, three teabags sunk in their box.

LIA LEFT FOR THE SHOP AT THE GARAGE. A tin of soup would do, with some pasta mixed in. Maybe enough for another night. Three cars were parked at the pumps in the forecourt and the old lady on the till served a queue. She was friendlier than the blonde girl with big eyelashes who usually worked evenings. Lia bought a coffee from the machine. On the shelves at the back of the shop were loaves, strong with the smells of dough and yeast, the way her mother used to bake. The bananas were brown and most of the apples were bruised. But it didn't matter. No-one stopped here for fruit. Better choices and fresher produce at Sweeney's on the way into town.

A globed mirror skeined a grey light as someone swung in. Him. Him with the dog. Except the dog was tied up outside. But him. His short jacket was matted and dulled as if left a long time in the sun. It had a texture like sacking or something expensive, though he kept the same shoes and had the same beard. His hair was longer and tangled, mad, as if he had been sleeping out. She wondered where. Where had he gone unbeknownst to her? He was all long strides, looking at the shelves, holding a so-called shopping bag for life. He passed on to the aisle parallel to hers and stopped at the refrigerator, picked up a chicken, dropped it in the bag. She was about to say hello when he selected a variety pack of hams and a bag of buns and slipped them inside his jacket. He walked past, just brushing against her, and the froth of her coffee trickled onto her hand. As he moved towards the front of the shop he looked straight through her, his gaze as sharp and clean as a cut from a knife.

Hey, she began, I—but he was at the till.

From the display cabinet of rolls and cakes near the entrance, he must've taken a couple, for he said to the old lady at the till, Pack of muffins, thanks.

The old lady rang up the till and he swung out.

She should tell someone. She must. Except. The old lady might not believe her and there was little point. Lia replaced the tinned

soup and the pasta. She did not want the taste and had no appe-
tite. When she was a kid she'd nicked makeup from low shelves
at one of the big chemists in town until the risk of getting caught
no longer held any appeal, especially when one of her friends was
hauled in front a policeman and the girl's parents had been infor-
med. But to swipe from here was different. Something meaner.
This was a tiny shop, the only one around for miles.

Beyond the wide shop window and the forecourt, beneath the
trees rising into the sky, the man untied Madlenka. The dog spun
on her hind legs in a dance of delight and trotted beside him, off
the forecourt, into the evening.

Lia left the shop. Cars whipped past on the road. Barking dogs
could be heard over houses and farm buildings, over the ragged
tops of the trees, but the man was nowhere to be found. The air
had grown chill and vacant. She turned around, searching, lost. In
her pocket, among receipts for cans of coke and crisps, a stone slid
into her palm. She might scavenge every day, for leaves or tufts of
sheep's wool, feathers from birds that had taken flight in fear, or
strips of wood which curled along her fingers. But never enough
to fill her room.

The Architecture of Trees

THE ARCHED WINDOW ON THE LANDING, looking onto the grounds at the back, gave the best view. The tree stood, lopsided, leaning towards the brick wall, for she had dug it in quickly, hoping it would merge with the poplars tall as soldiers and aged oaks and chestnuts at the far end. The burnished cupboards gleamed like the violin she used to play. Or tried to, her fingers stumbling along the bridge until she stored it in its case with the green velour interior on top of her wardrobe, years back. She continued downstairs, dust motes rising like smoke from candles. The floor was shiny and sweet from beeswax in the silence of cleaning, which she was beginning to understand.

She passed along the corridor by the office and parlour where, the previous month, she had laid down her clothes to sleep in a trunk. Low, dark wooden cupboards stored the belongings of Sisters who had already made their profession. Low as a purring cat, she had thought. In the kitchen, the latch was heavy but released with a jolt and she was out, the garden spreading from the lawn to beds of vegetables and the distant huge trees. The watering can was in the same place, so she stuck the nozzle under the outside tap. Up before prayers ensured no-one was around and the blinds on the windows were closed, unless one of the older Sisters couldn't sleep.

The week before, she had yanked the thin roots of a sapling out of the Sainsbury's bag. They'd dripped like spun cotton but she had set the sapling in the shade of the wall, where wild pink roses struggled up, colourful as a girls' night out. She watered, beading the ground, darkening the soil with droplets. To anchor the roots, he had told her. The slim trunk was silvery and its circumference was an almost perfect fit for her hand. If the weather eased, this might be sufficient for two days. She was returning the watering can to the shed when a fox snuck across the lawn. She was sure it was a fox. When she was a kid, she had only ever seen them in fields, but they challenged everywhere, nosing their ginger flare through brambles, interlopers on roads and down the streets beyond the walls.

The next morning, in the laundry, she bundled sheets into two washing machines and folded the dry ones. Opposite Sister Ignatio, in a dance of Elizabethan graciousness, Ann came edge to edge, corner to corner, scents of soap and detergent rising from the fabric until a washing machine clicked to a stop and she heaved the damp load into a basket.

Will you hang this out, please, Ann? Sister Ignatio gathered the loose pegs and slipped them into the bag. While the weather's good.

Ann carried the load and laid it on the lawn, picking up a nightdress, vests, robes. She went back and forth, collecting veils, gowns, socks and other undergarments. In the distance she could hear the murmur of cars, taxis, vans and motorbikes, couriers, articulated lorries and trucks on the Western Avenue and North Circular, all the arteries of the city. A train rushed beyond itself, going north from Euston to dense terraces she had once lived among. Or the dark woodland tipping the edge of the dales, where morning mists rose from valleys delved and shadowed with the forests he knew. On the washing line, sheets fluttered like flags.

SHE AND JACOB HAD SLEPT on sheets so white, others patterned with diamonds, and also, his favourite, black. Black so useful, she had thought, on returning after the abortion, the depth of the black taking the stains. In the end there were few, and she had passed through those difficult days without him knowing, without her having to say more than if she had made an appointment with a hairdresser. She might have told him. Should have. They broke up anyway. His entanglements with a former lover provoked streaks of rage in her, in them, followed by squalls of silence through which they voyaged like battered sailors until nothing mattered and they found themselves in some kind of survival mode. Until she found she was pregnant. She feared she might split and shatter.

Music grew loud in the distance. Garage, like her brother listened to. Or jazz, floating, carried near. Pressing against her skin. Heavier, slower. At Mardi Gras, in Spain, he had called the carnival primitive and animalistic while she had loved the gaudiness of it. They had continued along the coast, warmed by the days, dust in their faces, unable to settle in one place, to agree on any landscape. A hillside town one morning. A village the next afternoon as the train taking them south chugged on.

HER TASKS WERE LAID OUT, laddered through the hours. Matins, Compline, Vespers. In the battering silence, the disconnect from phone and computer offered a new freedom and she was learning what to do and when.

Helping prepare lunches, she washed lettuces and plucked tomatoes from vines like jewels from a hoard. She sliced carrots while another Sister, arms angled over the sink, washed potatoes, the sun streaking in. So much bounty. Nineteen Sisters, though it seemed hundreds. The following day, washing up, plates and cutlery piled high even though it was forbidden to use a separate knife for the dinner roll. Someone should tell those who hadn't listened. Was this not the Mother Superior's job? Ann swiped a jay-cloth over the counter.

The others gathered in the chapel for Plainchant, and though she might have stayed in her room, she decided to walk downstairs to the office. The door was open and a laptop, case closed as pursed lips, rested inert on the desk. It was used mainly for the weekly grocery order. Quiet as a host in a glaze of light. An hour. A half. A few minutes. But she let the door close and passed on to the grounds, walking the length to loamy soil thickening with the scurf of leaves and bracken. When they had lived in a village in the west of Ireland, she had ridden her horse such a distance or more, cantered across rough grass to the ends of fields where a view of the sea flooded her vision.

Out of a packed ridge of dried leaves by the wall, a small crest rose and a hedgehog scuttled under the enveloping trees near the shed used for woodworking. Overhanging branches almost hid it. Ann pushed in the door and Sister Lucy raised her head, skin pale as flour, thin glasses balancing on her nose.

I've disturbed you? Ann said.

Not at all.

You're not at choir?

I have no talent. Music is wasted on me and my back is not what it was. Would you mind sweeping the floor? Sister Lucy smiled.

Ann gathered the golden coils of wood shavings into a heap.

Thank you, Sister Lucy said. I'll find a black bag later. She turned to the lathe.

Stubby crosses piled up by the wheel, such as were sold in the shop or sent to parishes. Darker wood. Beech and ash. Chestnut. At a glance Jacob would have known which was which and she wondered how much, if anything, she had picked up from him, for he had told her the names of trees, a litany as they walked the woods of Donegal. In the yard he had shown her a commission for a house by a lake. Arches rising and closing to support a roof. He would have the same, he said. Wood of great age on top of modern walls. Green oak, supple and eased, adapting to the movements of wind and storms and realigning afterwards. The ribs had been like hands in prayer or a boat upended, a Viking longship on its way to the next life, she had said. He had laughed.

THROUGH THE POSTAGE STAMP WINDOW she caught a view of the tree near the house, of roses climbing the wall as if plotting their escape.

Do you ever feel tied in, Sister? Restricted?

Sister Lucy threw back her head. How could I, when I have my kingdom here? She opened her arms wide and smiled.

You've unchained yourself from the world.

We're all chained. One way or another. And leaving the outside world is hard. This is why we come here, Sister Lucy said. Silence fell as she returned to her task, peering above her glasses into the whirl of the mechanics, the greased slivers of metal and cogs.

Ann dared: But did you leave anyone?

Sister Lucy sat back, her hands falling to her lap as the lathe ran to its end.

Believe me, there was a time.

Her lips were pale pink and moist. She blinked, readjusted her glasses, and leaned back into the work.

ANN WALKED TO THE HOUSE while, at the far reaches of the acreage, one of the Sisters in protective whites and veil moved solemnly between the hives. She slid up the wooden slat for honey and let it drop. The bees never swarmed or scared her, but moaned, a low hum, enticed back to their home.

Hours fell into place. The bell rang out at midday and in the evening for the Angelus, echoing down the corridors and grazing the rooftops, tolling against the shriek of sirens, the city.

Assigned to the baking room the next day, amid the doughy aroma, Ann helped two Sisters make the Hosts. The elder Sister mixed the thin dough, spooning it into moulds. The younger tipped the golden coins, smooth as light, into a heap while Ann weighed half a kilogram into a plastic bag and sealed it. The work was important and it was a privilege to be with them, even if only packing. After two weeks she was getting faster and not dropping so many on the bench. When she had done this, early on, the other two had smiled encouragingly until the seventeen packs were ready for posting.

THE NEXT TIME SHE WAS FREE, she chose to work in the garden, seeking tools from the old shed. Beaten up by the weather, panels splintering, it sat by the vegetable plot, a treasure trove of broken hoes, rusty seed sifters, forks and trowels, worn orange boxes with pots of seedlings and rows of empty jam jars with nails and screws like her grandfather's.

Sister Benedicta raked over the ground to set courgettes and potatoes. Her veil swept off to reveal a broad forehead, weathered, washed by the sun.

Observez les petits. She smiled, proud of her crops. She inhabited the outside as if belonging only there, although one of the other Sisters had said Benedicta was once a model in Paris; another had said an artist's life model. Benedicta's long arms were good for hoeing and stretching to high branches for pruning, but when it was time for prayer she downed her tools and marched off, her own time-piece, bound by little except what was expected of her.

THE FIRST LETTER FROM ANN'S PARENTS came at the end of the month and she read of her aunt's holiday in Rome. Her sister taking exams. And him. Her mother said Jacob had gone to Asia and caught TB; she'd heard the news from someone at work who knew a friend of his sister. Ann folded the sheet back into the envelope and stood at the window. Grass spread to the vegetable plot, crept under the trees at the far end of the grounds.

At night, when the others retired, she slipped down the back stairs to the kitchen and out. The watering can was not in its place. She scoured the shed. She thought she might succeed if she used a saucepan, so she returned inside and rummaged among the kitchen shelves. Amidst pans, she chose the largest and filled it from the outside tap.

The earth at the base of the tree was dry and crumbly. The bark flaked and leaves frazzled like hardened skin. She drained every drop and a ladybird settled on the trunk. She put out her hand and it crawled onto her skin, a bloodspot come to life and moving, until she stepped back and it flew off.

At breakfast, the hushed talk was of the aroma of Benedicta's newly delivered manure. Some sisters said the purchase was a distraction from prayer, others said it ensured one had to focus more firmly.

After Lauds, Benedicta asked Ann to help wheelbarrow the manure to all parts of the vegetable garden, so it could be evenly spread. It will give nourishment, she said. And horse is the best. She smiled as Ann pushed off with the barrow, up and down the length of the plot. I have told myself I will have this done by my saint's day, tomorrow. April 17. How easily the day slid in amongst all the others. The day they had met. At the end of their first year together, Jacob announced they were going to a cabin in Norway. The next year, they slept on a beach in Greece. She gripped the barrow for something to hold. The date rang loudly through her and always would; past and yet within, as all days passed on their round, even as she hoped to outrun it.

WHEN THE OTHERS TURNED IN AFTER COMPLINE, she slipped outside and searched the shed for a shovel. The oldest and least likely to be missed had a worn handle and a blade slightly loose. She crossed to the vegetable plot and slid a squadge of manure from the courgettes onto the blade, and carried it to her tree. A boost. A tonic, her mother might have said, as she edged around the side of the house. She dug in the manure, down and down, stamping it with the blade, but her finger caught a splinter and despite sucking and rubbing she could not get it out.

In the morning she held her hand under the warm tap in the kitchen.

Are you all right? Sister Benedicta asked, leaving a clump of parsley on the counter. How did you do this? She reached out and took the hand, held it like something caught in a trap.

I was digging.

Benedicta looked sideways, grey-green eyes wide, forehead lined. She sank the hand into the suds.

You must've used the old shovel, which is good only for rubbish. Her eyes burned sharp while Ann raised her finger to find the splinter gone.

THE NEXT LETTER FROM HER PARENTS was propped up in the pigeonhole along with the following month's rota which said she was on cleaning duty. In her room, she unfolded the pages. News of her sister's car. Her father on Jury Service. A coffee morning for the local hospice and the trawl of parents' evenings at her mother's school. Only at the end, a mention. He had gone to Perth. Australian Perth. Someone at the school said it was a five-year contract, another woman said it was for good. No-one seems to know exactly, her mother wrote. As is often the case, the answer is open, she added, revealing her own hopes.

In the afternoon, Ann walked the length of the grounds to the shed. She found Sister Lucy holding a slender length of wood to the blade. A candleholder for an order from Worcestershire, Sister Lucy said.

Ann lifted one, its stumpy end solid with whirls of rings in the grain, a writing of the tree's history. She said, The grain gives them a kind of life.

Sister Lucy lowered her glasses, peeped out, eyes red-rimmed with tiredness or looking too intently at her work, and nodded. Yes. It takes a lot to kill a tree. At least I tell myself so when I hear about the rainforests. She smiled.

AT NIGHT, the walls closed in. Ann needed breath and could not sleep but fell to tossing and turning. She was in a small boat on waves which churned, drew her down. As she struggled to stay afloat, flailing and trying to row, her heart sprang open and sprouted branches, limbs twisting upward and stretching into the sky.

She woke early to the pain of her chest squeezed tight and her pillow damp. She rose and dressed. She followed the path to the far end of the grounds. Glancing over her shoulder towards the house, her tree in the distance was a stray among the others, but taller, the trunk darker with the beginnings of leaves. It takes a year for blossoms, he'd said. She sat on a bench near a wizened stone statue of a woman in flowing robes, whose feet were chipped but with no indication of which saint she might be. He'd said his idea of bliss was being at home. She'd been the one wanting travel. She continued to the dark firs and thick-trunked ancient trees heavy with scent. The ground was dusty with crumbling leaves. The words of her mother's letter returned to her, the pitch conveying a slight tilt of the head as her mother emphasised a point. A science teacher, she always found clarity. Saw both sides of everything. Even in the choice of paint for decorating a room, she would consider how darker shades made space seem small, contained and warmer, while acknowledging muted tones increased the sense of light.

Ann walked into the towering sweep of leaves, her foot catching a branch. Bark lizard with scales. She might use this. Make something. Work it on the lathe, roll it against the wheel and transform it. She picked up the piece of wood and continued on, swallowed by the overwhelming branches while thrushes exchanged their early intimacies.

Breakfast With Rilke

THE DRIVER WAS NAMED KEITH. I got in when the dark green Volvo slowed because he looked like one of my old art teachers. I wasn't fussy, as long as he was going near London. He leaned forward and fiddled with the radio until high-pitched singing filled the car.

What's that? I asked.

Liturgical chants. In a setting by Byrd.

Who?

Byrd. He composed madrigals with a viol accompaniment.

Uh?

He was a Renaissance—oh, never mind.

Keith fiddled with the knob. I didn't say anything. After all, it was his car. When he stopped for petrol, a skinny blonde fella was hunched on a low wall.

He looks a sorry sight, Keith said. One more won't matter. Keith spoke with a northern accent which was, he'd told me emphatically, from Salford, not from Manchester.

But one more did matter to me. I had to push my seat forward and pull my backpack off the other. When I looked up, a pale face with light hair peered in through the window.

You going to London? the boy asked in an accent more foreign than Keith's.

Yes, Keith said.

Thank you. The boy stood with his backpack in his arms, like a child.

Come a long way?

From Coventry.

Coventry?

Keith was a soft touch, saying how difficult it is for kids these days with no jobs. I wanted to say: I don't need your nice, clean sympathy. Give us the cans. Hand over the Mars bars.

Yes. I liked it. I went for the congress. The boy smiled. In Warsaw. For world peace. For science students.

He had lightly tanned skin and ears curving like shells. As he spoke I recognised he was German. I'd met Germans the summer I went cycling with Sorcha around Lough Erne.

I have seen many interesting places since I came here, he said. Birmingham, Walsall, and also I have been to Stratford.

Shakespeare's country, Keith said. I worked that way once.

I haven't been anywhere in England, I hated admitting.

What part of Germany are you from? Keith asked. West? East?

The old East. Leipzig. But I travel the whole summer. I have been to France, to Spain. Later I am going to Sweden and Denmark. I won a scholarship to see Europe. I am Marek.

Marek put forward his hand to shake mine.

Patsy.

He frowned.

Short for Patricia, I offered.

What place is this? he asked as we passed endless fields of wheat.

Northamptonshire, Keith said.

Northamptonshire went by in its sameness. Keith asked Marek about German history and the future, while England rolled out all around us. It was warm for October. Floods of fallen leaves spread over fields. To the side of the road, tall trees reared up, their branches colliding and full before a sprawl of warehouses. I wanted to say, Look, we are as bad as you; poor design doesn't happen only in Eastern Europe. But when I peered into the manicure mirror in the white plastic sun shade, I saw Marek was asleep. His lips made a slender smile. I wanted to ask if he knew anyone who was around when the wall came down. Did he get a piece? His long, tanned hands clasped the strings of the leather pouch hanging in front of his chest. When we drew to a halt at lights he woke and his thin face jolted to life.

Where are you going in London? Keith asked.

Cal-e-do-ni-an Road, Marek said.

She's going that side of London, too, Keith said with a gesture in my direction. Aren't you? So I was saying, before you got in, she wants to be careful. Big city and all.

I'll be all right, I said. I'm looking for my dad.

You've lost him? Keith asked, silvery cufflinks catching glints of sunlight.

What could I say? We had a day once at the seaside when I was five. He held me on the back of a donkey. Last time we'd been together I was twelve and we ate a meal at the Europa. He was tall with dark hair, closely cropped, and skin a warm brown. He used to phone when I was younger and send me things for birthdays. But when I was thirteen he rang and said he'd see me, and promised to phone again, and although he did, I had to wait months for the call. And it came from London. He said he was doing art work there and gave me his number. I wanted to know more. Everything. To reach this big, tall man who had let my mum down. But when I tried his number it rang on and on and he never answered.

Industrial estates. Boxy old homes. Plain faces of warehouses in beige or grey, like Belfast in the development zones.

We arrived quickly on the outskirts of the city. Houses and roads and houses.

I'll drop you here to get a train, Keith said to Marek. Okay for you too, Patsy?

Carrying Fire and Water

It was as good as anywhere since I didn't know where I was. We unfolded out of the car. Keith gave us a bag of tangerines, the remains of an Aero bar, and some crisps. Then he drove off.

WHERE ARE YOU GOING? Marek asked, heaving his backpack onto his shoulders.

Sorcha's address was in my pocket, along with my aunt Kate's, but I didn't want to stay with her in case stuff about me got back to Mum. I couldn't stand her pinched, drawn face, or her seedy life with no husband or kids.

I haven't anything fixed.

I have not either. But I have a friend, Albert. We met at the congress. Marek fumbled with a piece of paper in his pocket. Albert might be able to help us, he said.

Great.

Everything was fast. Shops. People. But we found a quiet place and Marek phoned. No answer. It was twenty to seven. We walked up and down the street. I'll try again, he said at seven. He tried, but still: no answer. He was pale and strange in the dingy light. He didn't know this place any better than I did. After three hours hanging around aimlessly we still couldn't reach his friend. We walked down a tiny street of cramped houses. Outside a small hotel with flower boxes, we came to a stop. We could try here? Marek suggested. I kept this, in case. He pulled a wad of notes from inside his jacket.

We can't spend all that, I said. What about we book in but leave early? Like five? Before anyone is up.

The hotel foyer was calm with a deep blue carpet and a mock chandelier. We must have looked like strays but managed to convince the girl at reception to give us a room with two singles.

I couldn't sleep. My dad must have ended up living somewhere in the city. He and mum had married in Leeds, after he came over from Guyana. They went to Derry to be near her family and I'd be stuck there if Sorcha hadn't told me about the boat to Stranraer.

I was tired and raw when we crept out. No-one was on the desk as we slid into the cold, burdened by the badly packed bags stashed with the little holders of shampoo, soap, and shower caps. I was hot and sweaty from running but we had done it, though Marek said he felt terrible because he was in a foreign country.

At nine he phoned Albert again and got through.

Do you want to come with me? he asked.

He was open and more interesting than my aunt, so I said yes.

The paint on Albert's front door flaked. The door opened onto a large room with high walls. Albert was short with a beard and a smooth, easy accent. There were low shelves and a mattress on the floor. No-one at home had anything like this.

Coffee? Albert asked. Tea?

Tea, please.

Herbal? Peppermint? He drew down a teapot from a shelf.

Have you got ordinary?

Sorry.

Coffee, then. Thanks.

We sat on low cushions. He tugged at the cuff of his expensive looking sweater and told us about an empty house a couple of roads away. Marek kept saying he didn't want to break the law.

You can stay there, Albert said.

He led the way as we passed terraces, more grand and robust than those at home, with floral decorations and a kind of gargoyle looking over each window. He let us in with a key hidden behind a chipped terracotta vase in a corner of the porch.

Makes life easier, Albert said. More sociable. Upstairs they're Australians. If they get too much, you can bang on the wall.

ALBERT LENT US BRUSHES and we bought a couple of cans of cheap pink paint. We put sheets up on the windows, carried a chest of drawers from a charity shop, and found a wardrobe for mine. I couldn't find Sorcha's number, so I phoned my aunt. Her thin, reedy voice ground on as she asked about Mum. I persuaded her I was with friends. When I told her the address she said, A very nice area. Her accent had the ring of home.

Yes, I said, they're very nice friends.

This stopped her. I told her Mum had come around to the notion of me leaving. What a liar. Aunt Kate said she'd let Mum know I'd called. I rang the last number we had for my dad, a land-line, but the woman who answered said he'd moved on. She didn't know where, she snapped, and a dead tone hummed.

I SHOWED MAREK the only photo I'd been able to keep. Taken on a beach, my dad stood behind me to hold my hands up. I was a fat bundle with reddish curls. The sea was in the background and his black face was stark against it. Mum never told me why they'd split, but one of my cousins said he had a temper and there were always arguments. He liked going out and spending money. But he was a musician, he liked fun, he liked to have a good time, and his big laugh swept you up.

When I was small, he took me into the city without telling Mum. We were in a shop and a week later it went up in smoke.

So you are lost and between places, Marek said. The fine hairs above his lip shone blonde.

IN THE EVENINGS, I went round the pubs. I would come in at the front doors and scrutinise the sea of faces. Once I asked at the bar for my dad by name but it seemed the more people I saw, the lower my chances of finding him. I was searching for the wind.

I kept hoping to see him as we passed houses and small shops in the neighbourhood.

Marek and I went to Chinatown. A red car was stopped in the middle of a street which had been cordoned off. A police car sat parked in the distance and people were heading off in the other direction.

The police are suspicious, he said.

They want to keep living, I thought.

I lay on my bed, under the flaking ceiling. A bird chirped in the wide silence. In the morning, I woke sobbing after dreams of trees and waves. Marek heard me and came to my room. This will help, he said. He placed a book on my duvet. The cover was plain with only the guy's name and the title. Rilke. Marek said, Rilke knew solitariness and exile because he loved a woman but she lived far away.

He opened to a certain page and read aloud in German.

I waited for him to stop before I asked: What's it say?

It says: We know places like a little church or stream but we still go out wandering. We still want to go out under the trees and lie down, facing the sky again.

But what does it mean?

I guess it means we go on finding each other. We open ourselves to the future. Give each other another chance.

Marek had trusted a lot, coming all the way from Germany. He left the book on the edge of the bed and said I could borrow it. But I picked it up and handed it back because I was afraid I might lose it.

SOMETIMES ALBERT CAME AROUND and, after watching a film on his laptop, we'd watch the fighting in the Middle East. Marek was fascinated by the planes. Through Albert, we met Angie from

Glasgow. She had short dark hair and wore a New York Dolls T-shirt and was studying political history.

How can she wear that? Albert whispered. How can Glen stand it?

I didn't know, but Glen didn't seem to mind. He had an ease which reminded me of my dad, though he was darker. He told me about Dominica, where his folks were from. He said he'd like to go back. Albert's girlfriend, Janna, was Polish and fiercely political, so I kept away from her. She looked impish and clever, a combination of features I could not handle. She was more often at Albert's than the others but she never smiled. I expect all her political talk depressed her.

Albert asked what it had been like back home for my parents. He seemed to think it was the next best thing to a Western. I said it was only a place I lived in and I was too young to really remember. I never understood why he didn't do more studying.

On a rainy day, he caught me unawares. He said he'd broken up with Janna. I was plotting my way through the area. My trick was to stand outside the tube in the mornings, near the newspaper seller, looking as if I was meeting someone, when he turned up.

There's a really good market, he pointed down the street. And a great cinema. Have you been?

I can't afford it.

I'll take you.

There's no need. We—

I didn't mean him, said Albert. I meant you.

ALBERT RANG AROUND for a job for me and I landed one at the cinema as an usherette. When the girl at the desk was off, I did the tickets. With the French films, I let in Marek and Albert for free until the manager saw me. Not even a week's notice. Time only to peel out of the plastic coat.

I was thrown into Albert's company. He picked up dresses and shawls, said they suited me. Somehow we started sleeping together. I slipped out of the house to find him in the late evenings, tolerated his pudgy body coming down on me, his belly like an uncooked sausage, his few spikes of dry hair. I was doing this because it wouldn't last, because when he rolled on top of me and clutched my shoulders with his thick arms, it wasn't really me with him but some sodden piece of myself. He knew he was buying me, and he knew I knew. But I couldn't help it. He took me to fancy restaurants. I kept hoping one evening my dad would walk in. He'd be impressed and would take me home.

WHILE ALBERT STUDIED I stayed in cafés drinking too much coffee until my gut hurt. Once a tall man with a silk cravat and a dark complexion entered. He didn't smile at the girl serving the drinks, so I decided it could not be my dad.

One day, Marek came in.

Why do you spend so much time with Albert? he asked, bumping his bag on the table. You should know, he's had lots of girls.

He isn't important. He only likes to get me things. A beautiful blouse, a necklace.

Marek stared at me as if I had spat. Why did he have to be like this?

I'm not stupid, I said. I know what I'm up to.

He was grey and strained. I was more than relieved when he left.

THE SCRAP OF PAPER with Sorcha's number turned up. When I rang, I was swept back to the streets we knew, the school with the nuns, a classroom on rainy afternoons. We had arrived at different times in the same city. You'll have to come over to visit, she said. Her words were smooth and rounded. She had lost her accent, or was trying to.

Sorcha opened her front door. Her fair hair was cut neat and she wore a fitted blue jacket over her jeans. Her flat had everything matching. Even the coffee came in a cup with a matching napkin.

I've got a fella, she said, sounding more English. I've been over eighteen months. You'd want one after that length of time. What about yourself?

It's not serious, I said. I shrugged, not daring to tell her what it was.

I was held by her complete calm and pale, made-up face. She spoke, breaking the silence. I have to be somewhere by six. If you don't mind me changing. She ran off into the hall. It's formal. Usually they're in wine bars but this is different because Dave's firm've signed a big contract with the States. Her voice rushed on from a perfect bedroom. I followed behind. She showed me wardrobes with mirrors for doors and curtains matching the duvet. Light music wafted from somewhere. She went off to change in private. When she reappeared, she wore a long, black wig with curls falling to her shoulders. She had not mentioned fancy dress.

Your... eyes?

Tinted contacts. A surprise for Dave.

We left the flat and she dropped me off at the tube in a sleek, cream-coloured car.

Give us a ring and we'll go out for old times, she said. But not next month because we're going to Spain to a villa.

MAREK STOPPED CALLING INTO MY ROOM but I didn't let on I'd noticed. He started working longer hours in the pub. One evening I caught him in the kitchen. He was good at cooking, even making his own pastry. The way he used garlic made my head sing.

Albert came round, he told me. He said he cannot see you tonight. He's busy. Some kind of thesis.

In the morning, I discovered Albert's thesis. Her name was Ulla. She was tall and draped herself round his shoulders. I stayed in. The war in the Middle East rattled on. Marek and I watched families die or live amongst rubble. A woman in a black scarf, like my gran, cried, torn with grief. Watching the news was easier than thinking about my dad or about Albert. Everything I wanted to say had been said. I was beyond words.

Frozen pipes burst in December. We had no water for three days. The New Year crawled in. The roads had thick coatings of snow making all roofs continuous. I kept believing one morning I would see my dad step out through a front door.

The swings and slides were empty in the park. The tennis courts were left wide open. Snow bore down on the branches of shrubs and trees and clogged the paths. A track of faint birdprints criss-crossed the larger prints of shoes. Their indentations and shadows melted away as the day warmed. In Soho, a café showed a football match which everyone watched until the manager said we had to go outside. As we piled on to the pavement, he said there'd been a bomb threat against the shop next door. Crowds jammed the streets, old men were disgruntled, young men in T-shirts peered around to take what they imagined was a last look at the building. I saw him. Eyes black as sloes my mother used at Christmas. The most delicate ears on a man I'd ever seen.

Dad?

The word slipped out.

He fell back into other people.

Dad! I called, trailing him.

He paused under a solitary neon O. Framed by the metallic sides of a doorway, he gleamed wings. At last. Him.

All right, darlin'? Look after yourself.

A Cockney accent. The man broke into a smile.

I thought only Dad's voice had changed until I noticed the sliver of a scar shaped like a dolphin above the brow. The skin around his ears and nose were slack and the teeth had stained. The man laughed and I was not sure if he laughed at me or the whole damn moment of delay. In the rush as the police announced we could go back in, we pushed against one another and the man melted into the crowd. A purple balloon from one of the shops rose skywards.

IN THE KITCHEN, Marek wiped plates and laid them on the counter. While he cooked eggs, he said he would go to Copenhagen on his way home.

I have to get home by the end of the month.

He set about making coffee while I weakened and needed to sit.

Why do people travel? I asked.

I suppose to lose part of themselves. Parts which trap us. Or maybe because it is possible, and it helps us believe there is a future.

Marek dried a mug and set it on the hanger.

What's Copenhagen like? I asked.

Small, smaller than London. It's pretty.

He washed up with his sleeves rolled.

Where in London did my dad wake, wash, and dress? Make a cup of tea? Stride out through a door to meet the day? Beyond the street, sirens screamed into each other. He might not even be here.

I am leaving Friday, Marek said, as the plates piled up on the drainer. It's about twenty pounds to the coast. I can pay the rest later.

I can't stay here, I said. I can't stay around for someone I don't know.

If you like. You can come with me. We came together. We can leave as well.

We were tidying when I found the photo down the back of a set of drawers. Dad. I wanted to tear it up.

Don't. Marek rested his hand on my arm. You might want it later.

I suppose, it's all I've got of him.

I would not say so, he said, patting the top of my head.

He fell asleep against me on the sofa, his arms around me and his breath the only sound, except for footsteps running into the night down the street.

THE TRAIN CARRIAGE WAS DARK, still asleep, as we left Liverpool Street on the InterCity at half-seven in the morning. Marek found a place on the racks for our luggage. An old lady pulled her bag onto her knees. Two businessmen sat glumly while we wedged in between them. The air was cold even though the heating was on. Marek gave me a piece of cake and bought two cups of tea when the drinks trolley came round. The tea looked like gnats' piss.

I got Agatha Christie and H.G. Wells, said Marek. Real English. And these.

A bundle of tatty books lay in his lap. I took the smallest book and wished I could be like Marek, absorbed, able to read that stuff. He unwrapped cold toasted sandwiches from his backpack. Marmalade oozed out the sides, along the crusts. Keith had given us tangerines. He was probably in Salford, listening to weird music. Or farther away, like my father. Or like Sorcha who had grown beyond how I knew her, in her big flat. When I arrived at where I was heading, I would text her, let her know I had gone somewhere I wanted to be and I sank back, eating the sandwich, the tang of oranges bursting in my mouth.

Weights

A STEEL HAND GLINTS across my scalp. A clamp of steel prowling. A leopard. Or maybe a lizard. Travelling around my ears and over my nape. Up the centre and down. Slides and skirmishes. A scrawl, shaving off the past. The making of me. The barber holds my head and hair falls in locks to the floor. Swept under the folds of the navy cape. I push out and away.

All right, love? he asks.

My eyes are huge in the whole of my face. Nothing to hide behind. I figured this place would do the best job. A clean cut. No questions. No talk about looks or styling.

THE LEISURE CENTRE'S better than serving in a bar until two a.m. with a manager who looks twelve years old and has acne. They took me on no questions asked, only my NI Number. Staff lockers are boxy small. The trick is to put the key for one in another and get the use of two. A woman rushes ahead, carrying a sports bag and towel over her shoulder. She showers as her boiler's broken and a young Sikh man in an Irish football shirt scampers to the gym. The kids from the special school and their carers arrive at ten and the chocolate bars have to be hidden from them.

THE COFFEE MACHINE CLOGS and sandwiches need packing but left on my own I don't mind, not any of it, not even the swell of people after swimming lessons. People push out through the turnstile, tousled, rat-haired, damp with dangling towels.

Parts are expensive, a man shouts into his phone. Don't go there.

Girls with blocks of mascara and kohl rimming their eyes run in. Think they own the place and leave a mess of cups and plates. Wrappers on tables. Napkins on the floor.

Andrez smiles as he passes. He has black hair and skin so pale I wonder if he's ever seen the sun. He frowns and says, You look different.

Hope so.

I drape the string from a teabag over the side of a cup and pass it to him. My legs ache but I can't sit. No room for a stool this side of the counter. He doesn't have to pay. Nor for sandwiches. Energy restoration, he says, while I stash away biscuits.

COLD EVENING AIR smacks on the way home. A dry bird's nest lies on the pavement, shrivelled grass and twigs. I settle it among the branches, frail leaves falling out. My hair, a stubble field, was once a forest of stories. I scavenged the countryside when I was a kid, for blackberries or haws. Sloes ripe and thick. I bloodstained my fingers till I got home, when autumn rolled in bringing school and lessons. Lessons. And him. Tall and friendly in an uncertain way, with thin glasses. Telling me Beethoven rambled in the Vienna woods. At Christmas, Mum said to give him a box of chocolates wrapped in paper with holly. He said, Lucia, you're giving me a present but I can tell you really want to give me something else.

BACK AT THE FLAT I make a sandwich and go to bed. Music on my headphones fizzes me out. All I have to think of is getting up the next day. Even though it is Sunday.

I slug out of bed in the morning, rough cold. The Polish couple, the Iranian girl who works in the estate agents, and the Scottish lad who cabbies: all asleep. None of them have anything in the kitchen I can eat. No cereal and no decent bread. All brown or the gritty stuff.

Dubai Mall is shut but the window shows long black gowns with sequins. People in the Evangelical Hall on the corner sing and a woman wearing a hat decorated with flowers steps from a car near the Pentecostal Church, her turquoise suit shiny with threads and a fitted jacket of gold. The centre is so quiet, the slightest sound echoes, so I slip down to the studio. The door is locked and I have no idea of the code. I slide my card between the chunks of the metal locks and the studio opens. Newly painted walls, the long slide of mirror where I see myself bulkier than last time. The rungs have all the weights. Blue 1kg. Green 2kg. Black 10kg. Plates like knights' shields. Others are the pastel tones of eyeshadow. Saturdays in Boots. Slipping a couple up my sleeves.

AT THE END OF THE DAY, no-one's around and if I keep trying the equipment will shape me. Smooth and lengthen. Take off what there is. Or was. Lift and down. Lift. Up and in. My arms pull and stretch. Press and in. In and out. And out. Squeeze every fibre. Taut and clean. My tummy's flatter and my tits have gone but I don't mind. My legs are thinner.

Thought you'd left. Andrez stands in the door. You could've got locked in.

Sorry. I thud the weights into the slots. Sunk solid down. I was...

I know. He smiles and I can't tell if he pities or understands. Him and his NVQ. Though he'll be a good trainer. Got a quiet way so's you wouldn't know he was getting you to do things. Mr. Blake was quiet. Quiet hands until they reached. So smoothly it might have been the cat. But the gnash of his teeth. The crash on my lips. Clever. Telling mum extra lessons'd develop my talent.

ON THE WAY HOME near the railway bridge, a rat scurries to under-growth, its tail twice the length of its body. Alert and bright-eyed and unafraid. A muscly cyclist with a tattoo swirls past as a child's long cry rises from a distant street, softening into the evening. I journeyed down here by train. Fed on cups of tea and if I made enough mess no-one'd sit near. I got a man diagonally across the table but he was too busy on his phone to bother me. Couples lounged over each other. Old Welsh ladies yapped. One had a grand-son exploring the Amazon. Another a sister on holiday in Sardinia. I had a bag and backpack but didn't know where I was heading. And something was left behind. Something always is, I reckon. Most of my stuff. Music and clothes. I won't miss them but I'll miss Mum. Her accordion with mother-of-pearl buttons and sleek black sides with glimmers of a rainbow. When I was a kid, I used to press the keys and she played, balancing the squeeze-box on her knees, teaching me. She used to say I never could keep a song in my head.

I SLITHER INTO THE STUDIO when it is crisp quiet. The weights are in the same place but heavier. Maybe because I missed a couple of days. But in the mirror I am myself. I bend. Ease out. Lie down. Lift a plate. Keep one between my knees. Make the new shape come. Clothe me.

What you doing?

Andrez is upside-down. His knees are shiny but his lower legs hairy under his baggy sports pants.

It's not allowed, he says.

Sorry.

Only for trainers. Besides, you don't need to do this. He picks up the plate, replaces it on the stand. There's nothing of you, he smiles. Make sure they're back in place. I do as he says because he could report me. Don't mean to keep chasing you.

You following me? I charge, eager to take the lead he's given.

His face crumples to a laugh revealing straight white teeth. I don't know anyone with such good ones.

Wanna see a film or something? he asks.

WE GO TO THE CINEMA because he is keen though I'm not really interested as long I'm out of the cold. He lives in a concrete building near the centre where he has a big room because he was in care. It's cheap, he says, and a social worker set it up for him, so he's sorted. He smiles.

A hostel?

Not exactly. Halfway house.

His place is clean with a view to the park where tips of trees brush the sky, lolling branches rich with leaves. The houses opposite are elegant, like prim aunts, with a terrace with iron railings and, over the doors and windows, a band of white coils with faces.

I VISIT HIS STREET because the house calls me and I am drawn by the glass in the door glowing red and blue. Delicate lines trace the entryway. The windows are misted with net and the front garden is lush with plants. A light pink rose creeps across a wooden fence. A dainty iron gate opens onto a path of crazy black and white tiles. The person who lives here must love it. I lay my palm flat. To wake every morning in a house like this'd make anyone better.

Andrez says it's an investment for the girl he's seen, but she doesn't live there. Seriously dressed. Professional. He knows a lot. More than me, even though he's been in nine foster homes.

He says, Some houses are listed.

As what?

Think it means not meant to be touched. Not done up inside.

He makes tea. The shimmer of boiling water. A clutter of mugs not his.

He asks how I ended up here.

I tell him I took the train to the first place I could think of.

He says getting lost helps you find your way home.

WE SIT IN A PUB, in the only free seats, which are near the toilets. Antique mirrors light up behind the bar and there's a little stage in a corner. By nine the place is full of men, bellies sticking out over their belts. A tall girl approaches the stage and settles on a stool. Her tanned arms are well-toned. As she sits the men glance up, fat fingers around their glasses, waiting. Dark hair outlines her heart-shaped face, billowing out onto her shoulders. Her sequinned T-shirt is loose. She sings an Abba song and 'The Foggy, Foggy Dew,' words riding out into the air as a boat on waves. Mum sang that song and the low notes gather, rousing, reaching for me. The girl leans back, eyes closed, as the notes soar like birds, gliding, filling the room, fluttering over the old men in caps tucked up at the bar. She sings with a searing longing. She wears the song and loses herself to the words.

You all right? Andrez asks.

I was that girl. Something like her.

Did you sing?

Used to.

The pub is hot as more men enter, clogging the end where the girl performs. She raises a hand to press back flyaway strands of hair. We leave and don't return.

A FANCY ORCHESTRA plays for free in the park. I've never seen a real one. Only in papers or concerts at school with kids on the violins and clarinets but this will be more instruments. Drums. Brass. Silver flutes. At the front, cans are scattered. The sun spanks the back of my head. The conductor rises in front of us with his long curly hair and a Ramones T-shirt. He says they are playing a Hungarian piece based on folk music. The notes are rollicking. When it draws to an end, the conductor announces a piece by an English composer and a violinist emerges. A thin, awkward boy with an overgrown fringe. He slips a pair of glasses onto his sharp nose. Mr. Blake said I had potential and if I kept playing I'd be his best pupil. The press of the crowd smothers and the notes sear, harder and hotter, and the piece grows wilder as the violinist's arm moves back and forth, his body leaning into the music.

THE LATE AFTERNOON IS WARM and a man sits outside eating while Reggae pumps out its incessant beat. Mr. Blake. His long face and limp eyes, begging. The thrust of his words, Do you love me? Do you? Do you love me? Love me? I want to shrug off the memory of him but it clings to me like dried sweat. I want to wash off the whole of me.

I CAN'T SLEEP AT NIGHT and Andrez asks what's wrong. I say the sun affects me. He lies his whole length down on the bed, feet sticking out over the edge. He rubs my back, my legs, murmurs how we have over a hundred bones in each foot, and presses at my ribs. He says I am gravely thin and tells me he is pressing the metacarpal of his hand against my palm.

THE ORCHESTRA APPEARS ON THE TV in the lounge while I'm waiting for Andrez. Local news. A charity walk, a school inspection, the park concert. Notes run, triple to a clash, with horns and a harpist and Andrez sipping a beer. I search for myself in the footage but no-one is me and the conductor is in the way.

Andrez rushes downstairs. What the hell was that?

I turn down the volume and hear a thud. A lumpen shudder outside. Andrez opens the front door as three men, quick in the night, scarper from the house across the road.

Some blokes trying to break in.

The fleeing footsteps lighten as the men disappear and the gate swings on its hinges. Andrez calls the police. Two cars pull up and the policemen do what they always do, stand around looking busy. A van arrives and a man boards up the opposite house, bandaging the door with golden chipboard.

DREAMS CRAM MY SLEEP. I ride a horse of the deepest chestnut from the farm next door. The sky is lowering dark, thrown with stars, and in the distance the deep blue sound of trains crosses the night. A scratch of blackbirds rises against the morning light. I wake but lie there, hear his voice: When you play, brightness shines.

HIS SULLEN EYES had shadows underneath. Mum was pregnant and had to lie in bed. He came on Tuesdays after science last thing. I sat on the piano stool with the golden edges and he opened the casing of the metronome. The white front with the pendulum lying like a tie was exposed and he showed me how to adjust the tiny weight, sliding it up and down. When he wound it up for my piece after the scales and exercises, the pendulum flicked each way. Each way. I squeezed down on the pedals. I didn't feel the pressure at first. I had my fingers to watch. Had to keep busy. The notes were quick and might run from me. They could catch me out. I squeezed down the pedals and did not feel him. Or maybe I did, but Mum was upstairs and I could not disturb her. She had said this one would be the last. Unexpected, she said. The metronome swung, back and forth and back like a flag waving in changing winds. His fingers. His hand. Under the keyboard you could not see. He pressed. Sliding up. Further. Until it was all gone. My fingers ran with nowhere to hide.

ON THE WAY TO THE CENTRE, a front door opens at a terraced house and three little girls still in pyjamas dance out to the garden until their father shoos them in. At the bus stop, a thin, raggedy man reads a paperback. I've seen him lots of mornings. Even when it is early. The scratchy grass frontage of the car showroom has no cars. Only signs for SALE and DISCOUNT and SECONDHAND WANTED. The other shops have grilles drawn all day.

THE NOTES WERE RUNNING but the keys stayed still. Black and white and black. Playing me. My feet were somewhere else. His hand was warm. I played to block it out. Down and down. My feet on the pedals. The stave was a fence and if I kept running I would find a gap to sneak through. Slip through while all the time the touch was running, running.

I'M MOVING, I say.

The sun slashes in through Andrez's window, and treetops rise over the roofs like umbrellas of green. They allow the merest incisions of light.

You got a better job?

He stretches out on his bed, riffling through the pages of a ragged magazine from downstairs.

No, I say.

He sits upright. What, then?

Moving. Moving away.

Where? You don't know anywhere.

He lets the old *GQ* slip to the floor.

Gateshead, I lie. Rents here are too much. The house is too full... the centre...

Gateshead? But it's so far.

Everywhere is far but I like the sound of the place. I'll arrive with what I've got on my back and won't know anyone. Mum got the piano from the pub she worked in as the manager was throwing it out and one of the regulars with a van delivered it. I used to like its russet tones, like the depths of forests, and the fancy brass flower holders where candles fitted in the old days when women wore hats and long dresses and people sang at home.

Lost Children

TWO DAYS INTO AMERICA, I stopped off in Cleveland. I was changing planes and reckoned I may as well stay there. I had seen the war memorial and the new shopping mall and was at the art museum, looking at Egyptian pots, Indian vases, the Jackson Pollock, when I heard a voice.

Nice, isn't it?

A lanky boy with a flop of light brown hair and a T-shirt with RHODE ISLAND across the chest stood in front of me.

Have you seen the van Gogh and the Degas? he asked.

There's more?

Cleveland has one of everything.

He opened out his arms, embracing the scope of the paintings.

Everything?

Yeah, really. You English?

I shrugged and thought how I never knew what to call myself. I had arrived in New York a month ago and was heading for Mexico. I wanted to see as much of the States as possible. What did this make me? A tourist? A traveller? A bum or a hobo. I didn't care. I had left behind two men I had become involved with at the same time after it all got too much. Really, I was a scaredy cat on the run.

Sort of, I answered.

Sort of. What kind of nationality?

My parents are Irish.

My dad was, too, but my mother's from Norwegian stock. You visiting?

A leather bag hung from his shoulder. It swayed as he moved.

I'm heading for San Francisco and then south. A couple of great-uncles came out for the gold rush, I thought I'd follow their tracks.

He was called Ben and in computers but I didn't hold this against him. He led me to a field of van Goghs where the land was churned up and ravens flew overhead. We strolled past interiors: chambers which held vases or opened onto terraces with the sea slung far out. We left rooms overlit by glass roofs. In the museum shop I searched for postcards, so he helped me spool the stand.

This is the only city with a forest around it, he said. You should stay a few weeks.

I'd like to, but I've got to meet a friend in Texas.

Next time.

In the café we sat in a far corner, away from a throng of kids let loose by their teacher. They wore red backpacks and kept joggling against one another until the teacher told them to line up.

Over the clattering of cutlery on plates, the swish of the urn and people chatting, Ben admitted he was past thirty although he looked only eighteen. He told me of his mother dying of cancer, and of how they'd had a nice house but sold up after her divorce and bought a condo by the waterfront. Once it had been a cool place to live but since the crash a lot of properties were empty. She had not been able to work for years. She used to be the secretary at the largest Volkswagen garage in town.

We're lucky, though, he said, because my uncle helps pay for treatment.

How do you mean?

She'd die. I mean she'd die quicker. The charity hospital would look after her but wouldn't do anything long-term. He's a doll, so

I go south to see him every once in a while. We go to Atlanta for nights out, even though it's got problems.

You mean race?

He nodded and fiddled with a stick of sugar. It's still on the boil, he said. He took a slug of beer. It turned out he had some connection to me. He said his great-grandparents had left from Wexford, arriving at Ellis Island where they were checked for sickness or madness. And they've opened it for tourists, he added. Can you believe it?

What happened to them?

They made out good. He bought land and got rich. It's how my uncle in Virginia is a millionaire.

I've only got an uncle a farmer, another a builder, and one an undertaker. More chances in America, maybe.

Yeah, chances for everything. He smoothed down the peak of his baseball cap. He suggested it might be fun to go to Cedar Point for the afternoon. It has the next-biggest rides after Disneyland, he said.

Better than Coney Island?

Much better. You'll love it.

He squealed with delight like a child while I was nauseous as we ran from ride to ride on the free day ticket he got hold of through a friend. We rode the Thunder Can and the Mean Machine. The vibration split my ears. When we went on the Roll Around my body left me. I came out at the end gasping for breath while he laughed.

Don't you have rides in England? he asked.

Yeah, but I don't go on them. I'd like to, but I can't say any of my friends would be interested.

People come out here for holidays for the whole weekend, he told me as we drove back to the city. They stay at these places. He waved to the Blue Lagoon and the Lakeside Hotel, both with signs brandished in neon. Glamorous red. Gold. Electric orange.

I guess I could get to like it, I said.

We passed places to eat, casinos, drive-ins, and we made a deal. If I stayed on for one more day, he'd show me Niagara Falls, because he wasn't working. Over a blueberry pancake and cream at two in the morning at Perkins Pancake House, I agreed and he dropped me off at my small hotel.

BEN PICKED ME UP the next morning and we drove past Hudson Lake on the highway. It took four hours to drive to Canada, so we stopp-ed midway. We were lining up for coffee at the café when I noticed a poster showing the faces of children in tones of grey and black. The eldest was sixteen and the two youngest were both twelve.

...last seen in Oregon...

...went to school one morning and did not come back...

...known to have been going to California...

Where were they? Jimmy Tufts. Howard Jacobs. Mary Teale.

Don't think about them, Ben said. They've made the decision about their lives.

I don't think I can forget. There's so many.

Come on. Your time is limited. You have to make the most of it.

We sat and drank our coffee.

I can't stop seeing their faces, I said.

I know. It's tough. I guess you get used to it. There are always posters like this around. They might get picked up in time, by the police. Or they might head home. A person driving might even recognise them.

I hope so.

In some ways they're lucky.

He stood his spoon in the froth of the coffee.

How?

They—they get to live, to go places.

I didn't quite get this, but in the end I saw there was nothing I could do and I was unlikely to run into any of them. There was no point getting down.

NIAGARA TURNED OUT TO BE like the postcards but bigger. Spray rose into the sky as we walked along the edge of the drop.

The force of water is cutting back the rock, see, Ben said. And someone died last year trying to cross it.

They still do that?

The *Maiden of the Mist* passed by, below, full of people, going right into the heart of the falls. Afterwards we walked the back-streets where shops burst out. They were low-down and tacky but I was about twelve again and excited. A shower of light, a curtain of sparklets. Nowhere else in the world could a person see this.

We moved along the streets, let ourselves get caught by the stalls outside. Ben held up a Bart Simpson T-shirt with FAMILY PHOTOGRAPH on the back. On the front the whole family was fighting.

I'd never wear that, I said.

A present.

No.

Go on. He had paid the assistant.

Thanks, I said as I stuffed the T-shirt into my backpack, sure I'd throw it away later.

My pleasure, Ben said.

We walked through an amusement arcade, passed a girl with long hair sitting at a mike in front of a mock golf course.

...you get the red or yellow ten dollars for a full round fifteen if you wanna give the balls a try again the red ball in the left corner hole in one swing and you win twenty dollars, twenty dollars...

We sought refuge in the Elvis Museum. 'Will You Love Me Tonight?' played in the dark, cavernous tunnels where gold suits were displayed. Paste rubies and emeralds shone on a black jacket. Elvis' watch, guitar, and bracelets lay on cushions as if they had never been worn, or as if he had never been dead. 'Jailhouse Rock' began. It was too much for us so we escaped to ground level, where Beyoncé blared.

Nearing six, I was hungry. We walked down a street full of restaurants by the lakeside and he made his way to one of them. From our table outside the restaurant, the illuminated pink and green falls crashed in the dark.

This place is for honeymooners, he said, gazing over the terrace.

I guessed it. He had lost his girl. He had planned on coming here. What a dope I was not to realise.

I could come back for this. If I need to. If I get that far. I turned to him and smiled.

Would you?

Not really. There are lots more places I want to see. Where would you go?

Hawaii.

Ever been?

No. Not anywhere outside the States.

Is this true?

Best holidays I'll ever have are in Virginia with my uncle, shooting. Come on. We'd better be making tracks. You going by bus to San Fran?

If I can stand it.

The last time I went round the oldest section, the Mission, and took a look in at the cemetery next door. So many of those buried there are Irish. I didn't see much other sign of them.

Can you recommend places to see?

He shook his head.

I was mainly at the hospital, he said.

He put down his fork. The pasta sat on his plate, heaped under a garish tomato sauce.

I'm diagnosed HIV positive. I went there for treatment. Still do in my home town.

His face was pale, his eyes dark and tight. Under his T-shirt his bony shoulders stood out. I thought of the drips on the canvas we had first seen. I shivered inside but I didn't want to show him. His fingers spread on the table were thin. They had little bits of white in the nails, on the ones not eaten down.

Does it bother you? he asked.

I shook my head, hoping I was convincing.

That's why I can't travel much, but I want to pack a lot in. I've been to New Mexico. I love the colour, the vibrancy. San Francisco speaks of death, though I liked it once.

He laid his palms open on the table. They looked like the ravines and mountain ranges I had flown across.

I think it was this German guy over from Berlin, he told me he was travelling.

I said sorry, though I didn't know why.

Do they say how long? I asked.

They don't say anything. This is it. Happens all the time, even in Middle America. Look, don't worry. I'll give you the name of a place where you can get a great Chinese meal. And go to the Mission and say a prayer, right?

Next day on the bus heading west, passing fields and barns, with a country music station on, I saw Ben's eyes watering, maybe like his mother's, and imagined his uncle down south, who he'd called a doll.

North By Northwest

ONE, TWO, FOUR, SEVEN. Days pass to the twelfth. I drive to the hospital down the A40. A swing onto the slip-road, lights and a left, past a long line of cars and into the squat redbrick estate where every window has a different lace curtain, every house a car in front so it's difficult to park. I've grown to like the area with its spread of streets with Anglo-Saxon names. Erconwald, Ethelbert, Alfred. It makes me smile, the idea of old kings living around here. When I picture the place as a forest, a boy I knew when I was a kid comes back to me. He had looked after trees in the wood near my house and told me he was an arborist. I am learning longer words now, words the nurse teaches me. Hysterosalpingogram. My tubes on the x-ray. Nulliparous. Me, all right. Never having borne a child. And this last word, I spent months trying to pronounce until I managed at Christmas, repeating for the first time the whole length of it: laparoscopy. A long journey to understanding.

The last time. Evening. Fenton and I walked through the park, passing by railings and flower beds and trees in plumage. He told me about the beaches *back home* and described his new house by the sea in Dominica. He said he wanted to reconnect with the land of his ancestors thousands of miles away where once, he remembered, a green bird had swam under his open palm, feathers trembling like waves. I said sometime I'd like to travel there. He tilted my face to his and said, not *sometime* but *today*, and talked about flight times but they were all numbers. In the near distance cricketers played; a bat swung and men fielded lengths of immaculate grass in front of a wooden pavilion painted white.

THE STONY GREY WALLS of the old hospital are like something from a fairytale. A castle. A nightmare. A plump woman pushes a buggy. Two thin bedraggled men and another in running trousers and trainers walk by. Two-thirty. Visiting time at the prison next door. For the first appointment I drove down its wide entrance until an old man alerted me to my mistake. Mistake. Moya had called Patrick a mistake, but she snuggles him to her, as if he is her scarf, or, really, as if she can't live without him.

Another test. Another day. A different part examined. The sign says: WOMEN SHOULD ENSURE THE OPENING TO THE GOWN IS AT THE FRONT.

Going to put this on you, Ellen, the radiographer says. Then I'll inject the dye.

He can do what he wants. In this clinical room he reminds me of the mechanic at the garage I used to go to. A bulbous face with tiny eyes and a faint moustache. He told me off once because I'd let the oil get too low. Though I had been going to him for months.

Turn to the left, the radiographer says.

I obey and it is over.

What did you see? I ask.

Mr. Graham will give you the results at your next appointment.

Great. I scuttle out. I am not going to get anywhere. No-one is giving anything away. Either I'll have to find my own answers or I'll have to wait.

NEXT TIME, they make two cuts. One to insert the laparoscope, the other to see what the hell is going on. Or what isn't. My whole inner clockwork will be revealed.

The ward is quiet at eight in the evening. The Ward Sister sits me next to three other women also waiting for beds. Hanging around with my small bag and waiting to be told what to do is like being a refugee in a new land. Later I am led to a bed by a nursing assistant. I undress and put my things in the locker. Already I am looked after. Important. All these people running around to make me better.

The doctor on duty is softly spoken and Irish so I can't tell him how putting off having a child has caught up with me. He asks my name and age and when he asks religion I admit: Catholic. If it all goes wrong, I want to go out the same way I came in.

At eleven, a porter arrives with a nurse and trolley. In seconds I'm whisked through long corridors, past the big windows where modern blocks spread out. I am new, reborn. Eager for them to do something, to recreate the girl inside me, dormant for years.

Outside the theatre, three porters sit around laughing.

He's feeling ill, the tall one says. A woman would do him good.

He turns. Like Fenton. Or not like him. Bulkier. Broader shoulders. Fenton made me laugh. At the office party, he'd described skiing in Austria: how, as the only black guy on the slopes, he'd made a clear path down the mountainside.

Within weeks we were working on the same project, sharing graphics, checking out photo libraries. We liked the same music, the same old films: *Casablanca*, *The African Queen*. Hepburn looking so frigging elegant all the time she's living on a river. His mother was a teacher like mine so we swapped immigrant stories and I ended up wanting him more than I would have believed. We had a blistering quarrel the first time we went away. He wanting to hold out for nearly a week. Me telling him I had to get home. And the reason. Robert. Our words were raw and jagged but we made up, spending a weekend in Dorset where I drew him to the sea, nestling his head in my arms at night in the small hotel by the beach. Over weeks, his hands on the back of my waist scorched into me. But he looked up with hardened eyes when I told him we could not go on. His face in grief and watchfulness left me pained.

IN THE RECOVERY BAY, I wake to a bulky safe at one side: the blood bank. Other patients lie on trollies and the nurses in green gowns and caps are like porters, but smaller. My body is coming round, trying to catch up with the rest of me, attached to a screen measuring pulse or brain activity. Lines flicker. Oxygen levels. Twitches, arches, dips. My readings are edgy and disobedient. A tall male nurse chats to the others, all women.

Come on, one of the women says. You'll soon feel better.

When? I want to ask. Minutes or hours?

I'll give you something to bring on the heartbeat, the nurse says, as the screen continues to tell me about myself in a language I don't understand.

The doctor arrives with a nurse and a trolley of notes.

Hello, he says.

It was nice to see an optimistic face.

Did you have a good look? I ask.

Yes. He tries to hide his embarrassment at my openness.

So what is it? Are my tubes blocked?

Your ovaries aren't working.

You mean never?

All the times Robert and I had grappled with each other in the middle of the month, in frantic efforts. All wasted.

Not for a while, he says.

It's quite usual, the nurse says. Sometimes they go to sleep.

I see myself asleep for years, waking up old and withered like Rip van Winkle.

Mr. Graham will prescribe something to get them going.

I hope it's soon, I say.

What I mean is: I hope he knows I cannot afford another six weeks hanging around while my body does nothing.

He moves off to the lady at the next bed, tending to her with his soothing voice.

OVER THE FOLLOWING DAYS, the tiny cuts become the black kiss of a stitch. Swift and innocent, even when it goes, I will remember the laparoscopy, long after I can pronounce the term.

I ring into work with a cold, watch films rewind, think about new subscriptions to channels I'll never watch, until Moya phones to ask if she can call by with her boys. She is exhausted from shopping. As soon as I open the door, Kevin and Daniel run in and hurl themselves onto the carpet. Patrick toddles after them.

What about going outside, boys? I ask. I've got a ball. I manage to make myself heard.

Ball! Daniel shouts. We'll play football. Watch me!

Okay, says Moya. But coats. It's cold.

No!

Come on, *it's cold*. Do them up.

The boys rush out the back, leaving behind an almost tangible quiet.

A good thing you and Robert haven't done much with the garden, Moya says.

Her hair is thick and luscious with curls from motherhood. Curls and sons. What else could a girl want? She slouches over to the new sofa and sits.

This is comfy, she says.

I should think so. It cost almost a thousand quid, I say.

So how are things? she asks, no longer tiptoeing around the obvious. What is it? Chemistry or plumbing?

I'm not ovulating.

That's nothing these days, she says.

We chat about her boys and their school while they run around in the garden. I bring out plates of sandwiches and a special treat, a cake in the shape of a steam engine.

I'll call the boys in, I say. They'll soon demolish that lot.

The boys rumble in, hot and red with running.

Wassat? Kevin points with his fat finger.

It's a train. D'you like it?

What? Train?

Is it so unlike one? I had spent all yesterday afternoon constructing the cake from Swiss rolls and square blocks of sponge. Finding the right sweets and liquorice was a job in itself. But it looks good. A glamorous engine going nowhere.

This part is the driver's seat, I say as they dive into biscuits while sandwiches are abandoned in broken pieces. They bunch up next to each other around the table. I cannot work out why they have not spread along. Must be to do with wanting to be conspiratorially together. Daniel, the eldest, has a big wide face like his father. Kevin is fragile and blonde. Maybe he takes after the milkman, I'd once joked to Moya. We laughed. Kevin is stocky like our cousin on a farm and Patrick has a broad forehead and blue eyes. Carrying the family with them. I have nothing to hand. Not my own likeness, nor that of Robert.

Don't like salad cream, Daniel announces.

Kevin chimes in, repeating him.

Do you want bread and butter on its own? Or with jam? I offer a plate.

Jam!

They'll have you jumping up and down all the time, Moya says. Sit and eat.

She tucks into a chicken sandwich, mayonnaise squeezing out around the edges. She is plump and getting plumper. Hasn't worked for years, not done paid work outside the home, though she says she wants to. When I'd suggested temping she shifted uneasily and paused. She says she loves being home, phoning friends, running up bills. Once she admitted she'd had a bill come to more than £200. I'd felt instantly sorry for Pat, all day on a building site.

The boys finish eating. Crumbs and crusts of cake litter the table. Globules of chocolate from the train spatter the carpet.

Can we go out again? Kevin asks.

Out? I glance to the window at the encroaching night.

Football, Daniel says.

Football. Boys never tire of kicking a ball.

It's your house, Moya says.

We go out at night at home, Kevin says in a sing-song voice.

Do you?

Yes, Daniel assures me.

Let them, Moya says. We'll get some quiet.

I open the back door and the boys roar into the late evening. Time was on their side even as they tried to pack in so much: kicking a ball, examining the bushes, playing around the birdbath. Their movements had all the energy of the very young.

I SHOULD NOT have gotten involved. Not that I meant to. If Fenton hadn't gone back home, it would have been more messy. He saved me that at least. Saved himself. I'd wanted him but I wanted both things. Easy to start, with Robert away on business, though he nearly caught me.

Who is it? he asked, finding me on the phone.

Only a work thing. A conference. I had to check parking.

I clicked off. Parking. The kind of parking we were doing between the sheets made me smile. I had loved Fenton's long limbs around my own. How easily Robert believed. When he had rung me from Belgium, I'd said: I've pruned the roses, cleaned the car, and had a look around a garden centre the other day. I knew this would please him.

CHRIST, THE NOISE. Moya shrinks onto the sofa as footsteps fall.

Kevin stands at the back door shouting and Daniel follows him in. I walk onto the lawn. The neighbour's property is intact and their greenhouse shimmers in the security light.

We want a sheet, Daniel says.

Why? I ask, coming in.

Ghosts. Want to play ghosts.

They get up to all kinds of things, Moya says. Drives me mad.

We put it over our heads and play in the garden, Kevin says.

Yeah, Daniel agrees, in case I haven't got the message.

We run around and make funny noises. Kevin demonstrates: *Oooh oooh oooh.*

I know all about ghosts. How they hang around and screw up your life, making noise when you don't want them to, never letting go.

I'll have a look, I say, going upstairs to the spare room where we left the sheets from decorating.

Draped from head to toe, the boys run out into the garden, screeching and jumping on the flowerbeds and shrubs. They run like puppies into the dark.

His face. Those eyes. Echoing loss. My tummy at the window pushes the tender place which once Fenton's hand passed over. The first time at his house after work, he trapped me on leaving. In the doorway, moving me to the wall, he pressed his lips to mine. An invitation, but a gentle one. Brief but illicit. I should have told him I was married. But he said he had some scripts he wanted to give me. Old movies: *North By Northwest*, *Chimes at Midnight*. So I called round and carried them with me like treasure, out of the small passageway of his flat, into my days and still had them.

The Stars Are Light Enough

FROM THE CREST OF THE RISING ROAD, as she drove, the school appeared. It sat, squat, oblong as a warehouse, in the mouth of the bay, like a mistake. Under a lilting grey sky, she came over the hilly bog and its spray of gorse and lavender. So much sky, so few houses. How did anyone live here? She swept past Corrigan's garage with the shed of a funeral home next door, past the café in the one thatched cottage for miles around, past the surf shop: closed. But this quiet place could hold her. She might last beyond the one-term contract.

The school foyer was untidy with kids, like any other. But also not so chaotic, for these kids were less boisterous than those she'd known elsewhere. The school had an eerie emptiness to it, as if the neighbouring sea had seeped in and dampened rollicking spirits. Most of the students were mild-mannered and polite, biddable and eager to please, distinct from the stagey, self-conscious city kids with their heads dipped to mumble into phones. Those kids she had encountered twice in succession, in her previous posts when on maternity cover. But this job could last longer. No-one was coming back from anywhere else.

Ellen. You're with third class. Shakespeare.

Oh.

I know. But they're lovely. Most of them.

Which one?

King Lear.

Maria handed over the texts and left, papers spilling out of her folder, a notch of keys swinging from her belt. Other teachers set off for classes, abandoning mugs, cups, plates of sandwiches, and so a silence fell. As a substitute teacher she wasn't expected to go to assembly, no-one cared whether or not she was there, so she may as well read, be as forgotten as a lost book thrown in a cupboard by the boiler.

In the classroom with its unadorned yellow walls, she pushed an empty desk to one side.

We usually read at our desks, Miss.

This will be different.

Like real actors?

Almost, she said, and directed them to shift the tables and chairs against the wall to make space.

They shuffled like starlings to one side, giggly with chat and eyeing her. She flicked through the pages.

We're still in act one, said a bright-faced girl with a red hairslide. Goneril's wanting her father out of the place.

Okay, Ellen said. Scene four? Lear needs someone bold.

Lagan, miss. The voice belonged to a chunky boy who pointed to a slip of a lad nearby. The others giggled and fidgeted. The thin boy slithered on his chair, pulling at his sleeve, raggedy with trailing strands. No-one else offered to read. His backpack on the floor had burst open, its zip broken. He seemed unable to sit still or follow a line of thought, never mind the lines of the book. She stopped him and gave him the part of the fool for he might dance around the ailing monarch.

You take this role, Lagan. And you—she pointed to a girl—take Regan. She would set these children free. Liberate them to receive these words.

The girl playing Regan was beguiling yet appropriately harsh. The role of Lear went to the chubby boy, who read aloud with an unexpected stolidity. But the fool was better, the best of the lot. Lagan's voice rose and fell with the waves of words, and even if he did not understand, he made the most of them, shifting and sliding his intonation, slippery, in the way a man might do when dancing between truth and illusion:

> ...if I had a monopoly out, they would have part on't:
> and ladies too, they will not let me have all fool to myself...

He had a clarity she had not anticipated, and if he was this good, she might marshal his enthusiasm to work through the play in sections over the following weeks. But in a change of scene, as she rearranged the chairs, he pulled and pushed a girl in front of him. The girl jabbed the corner of her book into his cheek. He squirmed and fell back, the chair nearly toppling into the row behind.

Lagan, Ellen said, sit at the front.

He rose, dragged his backpack to an empty chair closer to her, and glared.

We'll start again, she said, determined to scale the mountain. She would not give in to what she guessed he wanted. Slung out of class. Released from her demands.

In the middle of the sisters' discussion about their father, Lagan swiped at another boy who sat within arm's reach. The boy cried out, raised a hand to his eye, hurt, and the girls around him oohed and ahhed.

Okay, Ellen said. Enough. Lagan: corridor. You can spoil the play for yourself but not for everyone else.

After the class, she couldn't find him. She slipped down the corridor to peek into the empty classrooms, though she suspected he wasn't likely to be in one. Their sparseness held little attraction for her and must have held even less for the kids. She took the stairs to the first floor and checked each of the rooms, opened the facilities cupboard and the fire hydrant area, surveyed the new computer suite, but everything was dead and silent. One empty space after another. She peered into the music room where wire-frame stands forlornly leant against the wall and charts depicted orchestral instruments. At the end of the corridor, she tried the utilities room. Rolls of toilet paper and towels were stashed inside and the light didn't work. But a snuffling. The scratching of an animal. Lagan crouched against the radiator, the collar of his jacket upturned, holding himself as quietly as he could. By the glint of light from the corridor, Ellen saw his knuckles tight and white.

Lagan, she whispered. What are you doing? Get onto your next lesson or you'll be in more trouble.

He did not resist her grasp, though he shuddered when she touched him and he turned to take in her face. She was swallowed by a sense of helplessness. What had she done to cause this?

Come on. You need to come out. It's late.

THE NEXT DAY he hung around the corridor at lunchtime as she strode to the staffroom. Alone. Diffident. Until he swiped at the back of a girl who turned around and gave him as good.

Fuck off, Lagan. Grow up, can't you.

Ellen knew she should reprimand. Intervene. But the boy's eyes deepened, were sullen and ringed with shadows, and his hair stuck up, unkempt, so she let the incident pass. She'd heard other teachers describe him offhand as a slow learner, but his behaviour had suggested more than slowness, something less familiar, some-thing deeper, and she wondered if his learning needs had been properly assessed.

It took years to understand how to be with people. What did she know? She'd untangled messily from a man who'd been marr-ied, and never entirely freed herself of the one before him, who would ring late in the evenings to see if he could come round. She might muffle the sound of his voice. She might bury memories of his slouching walk, his youthful face.

At the end of the day, outside the office of Miss Garretty, the principal, Lagan sat and sulked. His long legs were angled as though they were running away from his body, in defiance of anyone who dared walk close.

AFTER SCHOOL, as Ellen neared the cottage, Tom lingered on the grass verge. He saluted, ducking his head so his peak cap nipped down. He looked delighted to see her, as if he hadn't seen her for an age, though he had gone over the ways of the cottage only the other evening, enlightening her about the lock at the back, the missing key to the shed, and how he could land her up with turf if she liked, despite the central heating.

She wound down the window.

You found the switch for the hot water? he asked. And the outside light? His eyes were bright and his cheeks had warmed with walking.

Yes. Got the thermostat, too.

You'll be plenty warm, though you'd need to be with the nights so sharp they'd skin a rabbit. The county council want to make sure the teachers stay. Especially the ones covering. He laughed.

Surely anyone would?

I'd say so. Once they're over the change from the city.

Kids are kids anywhere, she said, although she wasn't sure she believed this. The kids here *were* more amenable than in the city. The girls weren't as catty. The boys, but for one, weren't moved by so much frantic energy.

You need anything, call up to the house.

I will. Thanks. She wondered if she had not abused his kindness, for he had brought in a bag of turf, firelighters, and sticks at her request, but she had not attempted to make a fire. Is the bike in the shed fit to use?

It is, of course.

I wouldn't go far, but down the road the other direction.

It'll take you there. Good as any jennet or mare. He laughed.

And I won't be out late.

Even if you are, the stars are light enough.

Inside, she spread out books for marking on the dining table, with files and lesson plans. She turned on the cranky radio in the kitchen. It fitted to life and a phone-in came on. A quarrel over a cow caught on a grid, a river overflowing. More slagging off the EEC, someone saying they had benefited well financially.

After supper, she brought the bike to the front. The mudguards were orange with rising rust, but the pedals turned and the chain, though thick with oil, was steady. A chunky black weight with a hard saddle. Free of the car, she found relief in the wind blowing past, streaming over her cheeks, thrashing through her hair, and it was right, wasn't it, to be away from the city, knocking up against craggy stone walls, a wild sea at her back, roads leading over the bare backs of mountains, cleansed of the detritus of men. She passed a terrace of summer lets, and the wonky, red-planked house, unsturdy as a tilting ship, where, according to Tom, the owner was a fragile old lady of ninety-seven years.

A hotel spread, set back from the road and battered by sea-spray. The lintels were cracked and the wooden doors worn, but the place had a sign up, so she supposed people must stay there. Two cars nosed up towards it, even though the whole of the car-park was empty, and she was disappointed. She had imagined having the town to herself, mingling with the locals, finding out who sold fish, where was the best place in town to eat. Inside, a couple at the bar chatted to a fella balancing his gut on a stool, his cap odd-angled, while another, taller man leant against the counter. The couple spoke French. The woman mentioned Geneva. Her man laughed and explained in broken English how they lived in the mountains and skied most winters. In Ellen's one winter with the married man, they had taken a cottage in Donegal and after a long walk, finding a bar, he had ordered her a hot toddy. The spice of cloves had bitten her tongue. The brandy had glowed and flared and the sweetness had warmed her long into the night. The same would be welcome here but the barman was at the far end of the counter where a door led to a back kitchen.

Ah, he'll be along in an instant.

An instant. This could be anytime. The others chatted and she might have joined in but wanted to be sure to catch the barman's eye. He returned with a white teacloth draped over his shoulder like a slack flag, went past her and the others, and bent to search under the counter.

Excuse me, she said, as he fixed a swatch of nut packets onto the wall. Could I have a hot whiskey?

I can't. There's only myself. He rinsed pint glasses in the tub. She had a mind to leave but it would be too easy for him and she might get her own back and embarrass him amongst other more favoured visitors.

Would tea be possible? I'd love a cup.

I've no kettle.

His grey eyes were scathing, and his worn face was solemn as sculpted rock, dusty and ashen from shock, or perhaps exhaustion. But in those eyes, a wanting. And she wondered if he was married. Or if he was alone and had been for years. And in her wondering she nursed a violent urge to crack open something in him. With the man who was married, she had scaled rocks, fought against falling with handholds, searched for nooks to fit her feet. If she had encountered the barman in another place, at another time, she might have him rising upon her. Holding her shoulders. Closing in.

Orange, then, please.

He upturned a small bottle but did not ask if she wanted ice. She had an impulse to chuck the orange in his face. Tea would've warmed her when she wanted to be warm.

She sat in an armchair by the fire where a television was on. A commentator was giving the news and but for the ribbon at the bottom of the screens, she would not have guessed the TV was tuned in to Al Jazeera. Maybe here, way out at the edge of the peninsula, Al Jazeera had the best reception. But the barman need not be so unfriendly, she thought, when the aspect of the hotel, its views from the wide lounge across a wide bay and onward to mountains, would induce people to stay. And she had hoped to be drawn in, held by local gossip, to learn about the area. But if he didn't want to chat, so be it. The television gave her company, even if the reports came in from the other side of the world.

When a buzzer sounded from the room at the back, the barman hurried off. He returned in a fluster and busied himself with securing a new bottle of brandy onto the shelves.

The couple from Switzerland left and the two fellas chatted on. The price of oil had gone up. The man in town who hired out machinery had taken on a new lad. Good prospects for a youngster willing to learn. Ellen left as a news report concluded and the barman set down two more pints on the counter.

AT SCHOOL THE NEXT DAY, queuing to board the bus for an afternoon session at an arts centre, all the kids had more buzz. Lagan, especially, whooped along the corridor, slinging his bag from side to side, and with one of the straps he struck a girl from a younger class. The girl buckled and fell, her skirt fanning out, and took form as a star on the floor with the pencil case and books from her backpack scattered around her.

The boy ran.

Lagan! Unable to let it slide this time.

He turned at the call of his name. She glared.

What d'you think you're doing? Get back here.

Her voice hit the ceiling and the other kids in the corridor shifted out of the way to let him pass. But Miss Garretty turned a corner and came up behind him and clutched his shoulder. Lagan, she said. She must have heard Ellen's surprised shout, must have rushed to the source. Lagan! He slipped out of Miss Garretty's grasp, turned to face her and kicked the air. Lagan, you don't do that. Come to my office and you'll not be away on the visit this afternoon. Her voice was hard as glass, the way it had to be to enforce authority, especially for a woman. Miss Garretty was slender but had a commanding presence, with a swiftness and precision to her step. Dedication hung around her like a sharp aura. One of the teachers had said she had been a driving force behind establishing the school in such an isolated locality and Ellen could see how Miss Garretty had succeeded. Lagan stopped, and wilted under her glare.

The rest of the class stomped onto the bus and clattered in to belt up. At the arts centre, the kids pored over displays from the Neolithic age: earthenware, knapped stones, and knives laid bare when the deserted houses were excavated. The guide was a little fella in a check shirt with a bowtie and a ready smile, full of historical details and unfunny jokes about the easy life of the nomads. They rarely ate meat, he said. Pretty trendy, eh?

The kids shuffled past the glazed display cabinets, their dreamy eyes reflected in the glass. The boys were intrigued by arrowheads; the girls by wicker baskets. Pale stone pots stood like ghosts with rounded sides. The necks were dark pools of emptiness, or rather not emptiness but immense knowing. The knowledge of ages. All those centuries past. Lagan. His hunched form. His eyes full of questions or was it answers. She did not even know whose class he was actually in, as the lesson on *Lear* had brought together all the students in his year.

The drive back meant they arrived at school after everyone else had left and the carpark was empty. In the staffroom a teacher from the upper classes sat marking papers at the long table. Ellen was about to go home when Miss Garretty came in.

You won't have heard about Lagan.

Lagan?

He's bolted. I had him sitting outside my office and he took it upon himself to chase off. He's not on the school site and everyone's out searching.

The day fell upon Ellen and her legs ached. If she hadn't drawn attention to the boy, let him wander away down the corridor. If she had dealt with him herself, on her own time.

I rang his dad, Miss Garretty said, as soon as we were sure he wasn't on the premises. His mother, too. But she's in Dublin. Has a couple of boutiques there and didn't sound inclined to rush down.

It'd take a big crisis to shift that one, said the teacher at the table. I'd wonder if she's ever around. I mean, properly around. Ellen recognised the speaker as the bulky man who oversaw PE and RE classes. His shirt ruffled over his trousers and his thick hair was lank with sweat from a busy day. Lagan, he said, is the runt of the litter, after three girls. Of course they've grown and moved off. Melbourne. London. No interest in their old man's business and I doubt he'd leave it to the lad.

Miss Garretty stood at the window. We've searched all over, she said. The sea beyond the glass spilled towards them and receded. I'm exhausted and I've only done the school premises. And we've the inspectors due any week. I have to log this. I'll be in my office, she said and left.

Neighbours are out looking, the other teacher said. Fishermen, too. They know the currents. But Garretty wants me here in case anyone rings in.

Through the window, beyond the field at the back of the school, past the sheds, the bins, the art room, Ellen saw tiny torches flickering like insects all in a line. She might have saved Lagan. Directed him to more plays or reading. Or found the driving force inside him. His deepest buried interests.

He's caused a lot of worry, said the other teacher. As he has before. Garretty thought she'd got him sorted. But you never know, do you, with kids?

Lagan would have been warned and the school would have worked out sanctions but he had tried the limits of acceptable conduct. Ellen thought she should have let the incident ride. What did it matter if a girl was accidentally pushed in the corridor, when the kids bumped and knocked each other all the time? She had been overeager to show off her newly won authority, which really she had little of. Foolish. Unthinking. She'd been impulsive in casting him out. Pushed him over the edge. The school knew and had known for months what was best, while she was only a blow-in. Would she fit in? Was there room?

I should go out, she said. She wondered if Tom had joined in the effort, running over fields with a stick and his dog.

No. Don't. There's plenty out already.

But I feel useless.

Best to feel useless in here without the danger of getting lost. You don't know the area and we don't want to lose any more.

So they sat at the table and Ellen pretended to mark books while often rising to look out the window. At nearly eight, Miss Garretty came in to announce Lagan had been found. She called Ellen into her office to help compile her report.

Where was he? Ellen asked.

On nearby land. In a shed, sitting, humming to himself.

What will happen to him?

He might be referred to a special unit.

A different school?

Maybe. Somewhere smaller perhaps. This is another incident to log, which contributes to the decision. I'm sorry I have to do this. I have been patient with him and we've tried hard to keep him.

Would he have to live there? I mean, leave his father?

It depends. Not necessarily. Maybe he'll have to travel further.

Garretty was shedding him like a skin, Ellen realised, and so was she. Or tossing him aside like trouble, like a tumbled sheet she'd entangled with at night. She wondered if this incident meant she'd be deemed ineffective. If she had let him down.

Miss Garretty made phone calls. Lagan's father didn't answer at first. His mother didn't answer either. His father only picked up on the third attempt. This night of long waiting wasn't at an end. Miss Garretty told Ellen to make herself a cup of tea in the staff-room and asked if Ellen would make one for her as well.

Nearer on to ten, as Ellen was preparing to leave, she heard footsteps clicking down the corridor, towards the main entrance, with other steps of a shuffling pace. Ellen poked her head through the staffroom door to find Miss Garretty walking towards her with Lagan to one side, skinny, slinking along, and, to the other side, his father. Out from behind the bar he seemed smaller, wearied, drawn into himself. Lear, Ellen thought, and his fool, cast to the mercy of an uncaring world. Heading for the coast. Waves breaking out in the night. She wanted to run and draw them back, for she had banished the boy. Far from the kingdom of the school's offerings, what would he become but lesser, lost?

His father recognised her as they passed. Oughtn't he be flinging a cloth over his shoulder and ignoring people he didn't know? She saw in his eyes a flicker of awareness, a memory of the night before, and he looked older. His brow furrowed and his high cheekbones caught in the corridor light. He turned away, slung an arm around the boy's shoulders as a tautness coursed through his limbs, as if a shiver of energy surged into him from below. She might never return to the hotel, she thought, but knew she would always see him: his face etched with burdens, worries for his wayward daughters, aimless people like her hounding on his boy. He would be with her, would never leave.

The Love Object

HE DOESN'T SEE ME and can't tell how I feel, and tonight when he lies down he won't think of me or the others, though maybe he will and maybe we do mean more to him than the bunch of teenagers he has to look after. We are kids who cannot clean potatoes, so he shows us how, peel coiling off like clothes falling from bodies, creamy and thick, his fingers entwined. He cuts chunks and throws them into the pan of fat where bubbles gallop and spring. It is evening and he has won us over, hands down, by letting us play music while Clemmie lays the table because she's not so clumsy. We gather round while steam rises from the potatoes and his steel grey eyes soften. Finan says he will buy brushes and paint the walls, but when it comes to it the lads aren't interested, though I am and would paint every wall in the house with him. What does he do in his free time, when he must be glad to be shot of us? Hayley is tall and leggy and keeps overdosing. Clemmie keeps running off to her uncle's. Plus there's Steven and others who only show up for short stays.

IN THE VISITING ROOM, with the TV volume down, I can read my magazines. It wouldn't be so bad if there was someone to talk to but everyone comes with their suitcase of problems. They act big in the hope they'll get chucked out or moved on. They think they'll have their own room and a bigger television. It's not worth it, because I've been elsewhere and this place, never mind the shitty carpets and bulging sofas, has central heating. A person can start to feel looked after in this warmth.

Aelish? Anna says. You should be at school. Didn't Finan call you? Why didn't you go?

Didn't fancy it.

I didn't fancy school but I had to go.

Yeah and look where it got you, I dare not say.

Anna flicks through files. A shabby pink one falls out.

Turnham High, she says.

I don't care.

I can take you in the car.

No-one is going to take me to school. Upstairs in the room I lie down. God this place stinks. Shit and detergent, cigarettes, drink. No-one ever cleans it. Steven is lucky. Soon he'll be home. His parents want him back. Mum says she's had enough, and my dad went off years ago. I don't mind. It's got the freedom, the pool table, the meals and Finan, with his bit of an accent, from the north like my dad. It folds around you. He's too nice for this place and I can't work out why he stays. He studied up there, then came south. He tells me he went walking as a student, over the hills and moors. It sounds crazy. All the bad weather. He walked miles into hours and shows me pictures. He wears a shirt with a hood. It's dark blue and if it wasn't so obviously his, I'd say me and it had a future. When it's warm, he takes it off and drapes it over a chair in long, deep folds. The pockets are downy inside. If I let myself, I could wear it.

Anna opens the door and doesn't see me at first.

Aelish McKerrow. Shift yourself.

I'm not going. School never did anything for me.

I didn't say you were. I've had a call from your social worker. She wants to see you.

Tell her I'm out.

I can't.

Why not?

Because you're here.

I grab my jacket. I don't want a social worker poking her nose into my business. I've no reason to see her. I've done nothing wrong.

I GO BY THE CANAL where I came with Hayley. The water is gungy. Hayley said she'd seen swans here, and there were locks further up. She said she'd like to live on a boat. I said it's not so bad at number thirty-nine, but she said it made her feel pent-up and mad and she'd have more room on a little boat.

I'm gonna get out, she said as she pulled her jacket close. Watch.

I thought she was screwy. Nice but screwed-up.

Outside a phone shop she was loud and full of herself, thinking she's big, because of the knife she carries.

Going in? I asked.

Been there. Look. She opened her hand to reveal a slide of three iPods. Nice, isn't it?

Now where? Steven poked his fingers right down the deep pocket of a long black coat.

The arcade? I want to get more stuff.

You can't. You won't be able to hold everything.

I said I was doing work experience, Hayley said, laughing, and showed her yellow teeth.

SO HERE'S WHAT WE DO. We all go to the park and smoke. Hayley says she's found out about a party and she'll get a lift from someone she met in a pub. Her face is smooth with pleasure. Clemmie drifts ahead, kicking a stone. She's always been better at listening.

Finan might be there, Hayley adds. It's supposed to be a party by someone who works in Grange House, you know the place for really cracked-up adults.

Will he be? Steven asks.

Yeah. Hayley's lips smack down. So this was how it would be.

What do you think of Finan? she asks.

He's all right.

You like him?

Better than Anna. She's had a charisma bypass.

Hayley laughs, lashes snapping fast, her eyes fixed on me.

I might get off with him, she says.

I want to claw her, spoil her bitchy face so no-one'll take any notice of her at the party.

I thought you didn't like him, Clemmie says.

It'd be a laugh. Hayley lets out a hideous cackle.

How could she think like this? He tells me about things; I know more about him. I couldn't bear to be with her, but off she goes to nick a dress. I go around the shops but can't think straight so I don't take anything. Hayley has smudged the day. I say we should go to the pub. We drink cider, lager, and shots. I feel sick.

We'll have to climb over the wall and go in the back, Clemmie says.

You'll have to heave me up, I say. I can just about stand.

Somehow we get down the road. Clemmie holds my arm.

We make a noise going in the back door and Anna appears in an old red dressing gown like a bedspread. She says Finan'll speak to us in the morning, making us feel like a couple of kids.

She tells him about us, the bitch. I feel stupid hearing him go on about reports and safety. I try to tell him it was a mistake and anyway how was the party? Did he see Hayley?

What are you talking about? he asks.

She was at the party last night. You must have seen her.

I wasn't at any party, he says. And in any case, I'm not discussing Hayley.

When we have tea, over salmon sandwiches, Steven tells me Hayley is sick. I don't want Finan to think I'm as stupid as her, so I come downstairs later in my nightdress. The office door is ajar and the light is on. I knock gently and inside I see he is in the blue jacket. I suppose he's wearing it because there's a chill to the air and the flue in the fireplace doesn't work properly. He looks nice with his thick hair all standing up.

Aelish, Finan says. What do you want?

If I could make him like me more. If I could.

You'd better go back and tell me whatever it is in the morning. I'm sure it can wait.

It can't. I want him to know. I'm sorry I came in late. I know I'm younger than him.

I'd rather—

Wait 'til morning. It's too cold for you to be hanging around at gone eleven, and I've got stuff to write up.

He throws me out. This is what it feels like in the dead of night when it's quiet and there's no-one about and the landing lights are off. The floor is cold under my feet and my long T-shirt flaps.

HAYLEY GETS BETTER and no more is said. Finan cooks, makes us wash the dishes, continues to sort out quarrels about the TV and tidies up. He leaves his jacket around. I'd like to try it on but decide I'd better not in case he sees. The next day, when he's off-duty, it hangs on the back of a chair. I want nothing else. It fits. Suits me nicely. It'll do for trips out. I take it and Finan doesn't notice. I shove it behind a cushion. That's why I can't believe it when I see the jacket in Hayley's drawer, the way you'd stash a packet of biscuits, or condoms, or a nice pair of tights. I sweep my hand along soft blue folds, gathering fabric. She's not getting away with this.

Hayley is in the doorway when I come out of the bedroom.

What's that? she asks.

Nothing.

Funny kind of nothing. What've you got?

She goes for me and we fall on the floor, her arms flying. She pulls, kicks me, and I punch her. It was his but now it's mine. I push her and she is face-down, whining. I pound her. I get up on her back and pull her hair. She squeals like a mouse on fire. I hate her. Burn. You won't get this. She wriggles away, her thighs fat and heavy. Stumpy thick muscles in her calves quiver, they're fish skimming a river. You'll never walk again after I've finished. She is on the bed doubled up. I get her in the stomach. She cries when I leave. Good.

She doesn't say anything later and neither does anyone else. Nobody would've heard anyway, most of the kids are out if not at school then around the shops. Pale, looking ill, she mopes about. People will think it's over a bloke and it doesn't matter. Even Finan doesn't take much notice. But he's hardly in the house.

Next day we hear he's leaving. Anna says he's got promoted and is taking over another home without a manager. I'm shocked. Blasted out of myself. How can he do that? Walk off. I don't know how to take it. He belongs here. He can't have any other life.

What'll become of us? Will things go on like they used to? I still have his jacket. I know because I check. It lies the way I folded it. Hayley is going to Ramsgate House, a long-term place where she can't keep running away. Clemmie says the way Hayley kept breaking up her mum's place doesn't help and there's nowhere else to take her.

I don't see her go. She gathers her stuff and is gone. I go downtown with Clemmie and two new girls and take them to the fish shop, to the bloke with flowers tattooed on his arms, who dunks his hands among slabs of ice. Petals swim and scales run. He dips and delves, wears an earring and a woolly cap. I don't suppose he's as clever as Finan. He's not as good-looking.

I CAN'T BELIEVE IT until I see the papers. Hayley was found in the canal after taking a load of drugs. She was barely visible except for the blue jacket, with all the crap and rubbish thrown in. They took her to hospital and expect she'll revive. I read aloud to Clemmie as she can't read by herself. She leans forward in the chair. I could tell her anything and she'd believe it was true.

I rush out, going down the alley, and there's a bare, useless part of ground which isn't even allotments but has a mattress and loads of TVs in the grass. The water is dark and seeping with strands of reeds overflowing from the bank. I see Hayley fall, her hands grasping, water drawing her in, lap-lap-lapping, loving. Little waves crawl and jump, push against the blue jacket. I wanted it, to wrap around my body, but instead she's got it. Got him.

FINAN'S BEEN AWAY FOR A MONTH but I keep thinking he'll come back to deliver a report, see someone for a meeting, or us, but he never does and never will. Memories rush. He drowns in my heart.

Walking to Dalkey

SHE KEPT LOSING THINGS. A favourite tailored dress bought in Paris. Two towels. A watch at the swimming baths. The watch had been expensive and Ciara didn't know why she'd even worn it. When people asked, How are you? she'd answer, Fine. Great. Though in truth, during the past weeks, she'd been losing part of herself.

In the bedroom, she sorted clothes for going to Knock. If her mother wanted to visit, she had better take her. She pushed her T-shirts to the back of the lowest drawer, along with embroidered skirts bought when working in Mexico City and a muslin blouse given her by a woman in Delhi. Thick knitted cardigans lay next to exquisite cotton tops from Macy's. She had kept the cowl-necked jumpers because her mother had offered them as the height of fashion, which they were. Once. A fashion of safety and reliability with useful collars and cuffs. Remnants of when she was younger and living within her mother's gaze. But amongst the open spread of surrounding fields in the west of Ireland, she would be able to tell her mother about the miscarriage, a small acknowledgement to herself she should be settled with a man in the country with children and Sunday lunches. She would tell her mother about Ned. Or as much as she could bear to unleash.

Her phone rang, battering the silence.

Mum? Are you all right? A fall? She sat to take in the news.

The voice: Take more than a bit of a fall to hurt me.

Of course. Her mother was fine. A childhood running across fields and ditches had done her no harm.

You still want to go? Ciara asked. To Knock?

I wouldn't miss it.

Her mother's voice was strong.

Before bed she spread Visible Difference on her cheeks. White and pure, the light cream sank in but left an unmistakable trail. It spoke of fields of untrodden snow, glacial mountains, and she saw Ned. He had planned the journey to Everest weeks ago. The light winds and clear skies lasting only the month were vital for a safe climb. She saw him on the side of a mountain in a padded jacket, possibly the Aran hat she'd given him, and dark goggles reflecting back the surrounding light from the big sky. She saw openness. The sea. A wide bay of tides which spelled renewal. Only a season ago, she'd laid with him on a blazing, pale beach in the Seychelles. In the evenings they had walked along the shore to a cove at the base of a cliff.

AT THE SWIMMING POOL the next day, the water soothed her shoulders and drew her down. She could hide in the enormous silence. An openness overwhelmed her while white space spread across the tiles announcing MEN, BOYS, WOMEN, GIRLS. It pleased her to cut into the water, be her own knife.

She swam as whorls of light from the high window played on the water's surface. The lifeguard, a tall, dark-haired man with a slithery body of delicious gold tones, wore tight trunks. He strutted along the two sections of the baths, the lower level for beginners with shallow water and the deeper where she went.

The Rhinemaidens. Three older ladies she'd seen the previous week gathered on the other side.

You really should give up smoking, he told me, the fattest put forth.

The things she did for him after she went...

Ciara cut down their side while they babbled like kids and doddled the length of the pool, ducking and bobbing in rubber headgear. The largest wore a flower-print costume. The other two were in tones of pale blue and black. They amazed her with their dedication, as they raced each other while she swanned at her own pace. The smallest stood at the far end, pale upper arms flabby like a sheet of washing. No-one Ciara's age was around. Most women were working or struggling with kids. The pool held the decrepit, the mad, the old, and truants and deviants like her. The totally useless. She should get home and do some work.

She swam to the shallow end where the sun splashed her skin and made shadows. Climbing out, she passed two young men walking along the edge, their togs smooth and slick. The tallest, with brown hair falling back like a jockey's cap, pointed to a girl. Their laughter filled the empty air under the glass dome. The boys dived in. The girl, long-limbed, wore a tan and a swimsuit cut to reveal the fullest extent of her legs. Her muscles flexed as she walked along and flicked back her auburn hair before checking her watch and diving in. Ciara could only hang back at the sin against nature that anyone so good-looking could be so skilful while also possessing such beauty.

The mirror in the changing room revealed her slim shape. Nothing to show. All gone. Her face was drained of colour with her hair pulled back. In the previous three months a lightness had filled her as she walked around. Until the blood on the sheets. She had been at a conference listening to talks about the social effects of the development of the city. She had been frightened when discovering she was pregnant but was torn apart at the loss, which came sharp and shocking. A new kind of madness took over.

At the hospital, she had waited a whole day for a scan, two to see a gynaecologist, another to go to theatre while women wearing dressing gowns and pastel-coloured slippers with diamante butterflies shuffled to the toilet and back. One nurse came and then another. She had to repeat everything, always to someone different who did the same things the others had done: took her temperature, pulse, blood pressure, wrote on a pad. She did not know what ERPC was until a doctor of about twenty, wearing a floral waistcoat, explained. Evacuation of Retained Products of Conception. The accuracy of the words threw her.

Just hoover you out, he will, a nurse had said.

After she left, Ciara realised when the nurse had asked if she was allergic to anything, she should have smiled and said, Only nice doctors.

THE RHINEMAIDENS CAME INTO THE CHANGING ROOM, slipping out of their costumes and standing under the showers. Water hailed down and stroked their backs. One had rolls of fat around her waist like a half-filled sack and another had very wide toes. When a shower was free, Ciara stepped under, exhilarating in the spark and thrill of the spray. In the cubicle, drying, the Rhinemaidens kept talking.

She went to the opticians, never the same again...

This dress, they changed it even after I wore it to the funeral...

Swimsuits lay in a damp pile at their feet. The women banged shut the metal lockers, shuffling back and forth between cubicles as they recovered their clothes. Kaye rubbed the towel over her arms and shoulders, pulling it across her legs, making her skin glow.

In the foyer, a poster announced the drop-in Schizophrenia Group met every week in the clinic next door. Ciara could join, for she had long ago accepted how she and Ned would never choose wallpaper together or furnish a room. They would not discuss the merits of different tones of paint. Her interior furnishings were the intimate knowledge of train timetables, platforms across the country where they'd meet, and strategically located restaurants not far from the stations. She had known he would not leave his wife.

She pushed money into a machine for chocolate. School kids burst through the door, with a teacher behind trying to herd them. They were loud but small, seven or eight. It was hard to tell, for kids merged together as the years went by so quickly. She stepped through the glass doors. Wasn't her mother approaching, arms wide open and full, her focus adrift with small eyes like pinpoints of light? An older woman passed by, into the foyer. The big doors opened and swallowed her. Ciara wanted to fold up, overwhelmed by the sense of duplicity. How could anyone else but the woman who was in her own home across town be her mother?

The next morning her printer didn't work. She did not want to drive through heavy traffic but there was no alternative. She drove and missed a turning but kept on driving. One street after another. Cars. More cars. Taxis. She was going east when she should have been heading north. Rail Freight International Parcels. Copy Centre. Flamet Metal Packaging Company. They all passed by the car window. Traffic lights. Reds, greens, golds flying past her eyes. People on the pavement looked normal. She had to try to be like this. The girl in a short skirt, had she ever been afflicted? Had the one in the black jumper? Or her with trainers?

I don't care about the past, Ned had said. It dissolves when I'm with you...

His northern drawl, richly dark, settled in her. His warm accent all over her when they escaped for weekends, where all her selves had fallen away like autumn leaves.

THE MAN AT THE SHOP said he would give the printer a run through and check if it needed more than a service.

Probably the heads need cleaning, he said.

Yeah. Right. The heads need cleaning. She had read books say-ing she should cast off unfinished business, put it in chests, dump it at sea, in a wooden casket with black hinges. She would have to keep throwing the boxes out of the boat into the depths for a long time, or else she'd drown.

She left the printer with him and took refuge in the new Marks and Spencer where everything was safely the same. Rows of car-digans and blouses, skirts, stands of jackets, jumpers and trousers across the shop floor.

Spend whatever you like, whatever you need for the trip, her mother had said, giving her several twenty pound notes. My own mother used to say there are no pockets in shrouds.

As far as Ciara could tell, her grandmother had kept a saying for every situation.

She bought trousers because they would not show torn stock-ings when her mother bent or a slip trailed. A lush velvet pair would keep her warm. They would hide thinning legs and protect against the effects of a fall, though she would not tell her mother they were called jogging pants. She bought two pairs. She would show some kind of responsibility while her mother's defences were packets of honey blonde hair dye. They stood like soldiers in the bathroom cupboard, with the sample shade, the colour of corn, recalling her mother's youth, baling hay with brothers who'd worked in the fields. Her mother used to take the canister of hot, sweet tea down to them, walking along the sides of ditches. There were meals to prepare when the men came in, as long afternoons crept by in the summer.

At home, Ciara folded the trousers into the suitcase, leaving out the brightly coloured scarf ready for when they set off the next day. Outside, slow traffic hissed. The morning had started chill but by afternoon the sky had warmed to a pink glow with a rising heat.

THE AIRPORT WAS all glass and light like a department store. They boarded and found seats without a fuss, but once they were airborne her mother fidgeted.

Mum? What's wrong?

I thought we got a meal.

The flight is short and we really don't need it.

In little more than an hour they were out of the tiny airport. It was impossible to work out whether Knock was a small town or a big village as they drove to the shrine. A large pane of glass spread out at the back of the church and a modern section extended to one side. Photographs of crutches and sticks hung on the old walls. Along a passageway, prayer cards rose on stands. Priests sauntered by, content in their own territory. Her mother bought a year's worth of Masses.

Isn't Mrs. Garfield's son going to be a priest? she asked.

He's got a girlfriend. I don't think so. Unless he's bringing his girlfriend into the seminary as well.

Her mother laughed, her face alive. Her cheeks blushed. Her light silvery eyes looked out from fading skin, smooth over her cheeks but ragged around her temples. Unnervingly, the same colour as his.

Beyond the crowd stood a row of taps, each one with a simple engraving of a flower or animal on pale stone.

Have you got a bottle for the holy water? her mother asked.

What about this? She gulped the last mouthful of Tango, rinsed the bottle and filled it. Water fell in small fountains, washing the light away. She hoped it was caught underground and recycled. It was a shame to waste such holiness, such sips of sorrow. Tears of God. The water might cleanse her heart. She had known the price.

Her mother gathered empty Evian bottles. These are better, she said. They're big. Someone must have left them behind. You never know when you need more. Good to have extra. She slipped the lip of the bottle under the nozzle of the tap, as sensitively as if leaning to a flower, a child.

Ciara supported her mother to stand until steady and able to wander around the gardens, the shops, the prayer centre. Her stick, tapping the ground, hammered into the silence.

What do you say to a cup of tea, dear?

I thought you wanted to go to Mass? Ciara could barely keep up: prayers or meals, tea or holy water.

I think we've missed Mass. It was on the hour. Anyway, I'm thirsty and need to sit.

At a table on the pavement they jostled others for space. At the side of the café, shelves held miniature plastic versions of Our Lady and teddy bear keyrings.

The previous year, she and Ned had walked the lower slopes of the Himalayas. They had squatted at night in a tiny tent while with torchlight he'd shown her maps of the surround-ing villages. He had talked about Kilimanjaro, the highest peak in Africa. He'd explained land formations and glacial valleys. On one of his old maps, they had marvelled at villages across the subcontinent. They had talked about themselves as well. The difficulties of weekends in small towns, remote places. But we can conquer this, he'd said with a smile. If we can't climb, we can walk.

On the pavement, women pushed bulky buggies and a ten-year-old boy leant against a wall, sucking a lolly.

This time of year, spring, her mother said, is best. Everything is fresh and new. And I appreciate you joining me. If you'd a husband and wee ones, you wouldn't be able.

Ciara's throat tightened. The day broke with a shower. People huddled under awnings spread wide over the pavements. Tables smeared as rain splashed against her legs and bare forearms.

Knock at this time is at its best, her mother continued, not too warm and not too many people so you can walk, even if it's not as much as I used to. D'you remember the day the pretty hotel outside Dublin was shut and we couldn't go in for a drink? We went off walking as far as Dalkey?

Dalkey. Nestled in a bay whose houses rose up over the surrounding hills. Years back. She had been working in Madrid and returned at weekends. Before she'd met Ned. Before anything. Soon she would tell her mother about him. If not here then later, after dinner, when the two of them were softened by food and wine.

It was a gentle evening with little houses perched on the side of a mountain like my old home. I couldn't do that walk these days.

Of course not, Mum. No-one expects it of you.

Her mother's steps had shortened, contracted, as had her own. Her world was smaller. Shifted. Away from the wild spectacular. Ranging mountains smudged against a tropical red sky.

And May is the month of Mary, her mother chatted on brightly, hands settled in her lap as she took in the whole of the afternoon.

The hymn came, the run of lilting notes she had loved as a child: *Month we all love so well; May is the month of Mary, gladly her praise we tell...* The words flowed like winds on a mountain peak. At school they had worn gloves and boaters. Mostly obedient girls, appearing never to do wrong.

Her mother shivered and pulled her jacket close as the rain brushed her face and seemed to make her younger, fresher, more optimistic. Now Ciara saw the huge impossibility of it. She could never confess. She could never tell about Ned, still less about the loss of the child. Not the one or the other. Not here. Or anywhere.

She would work at becoming new. Start again. Enjoy being out in the world. Belong and join in as her mother had, flourishing amongst people in new places. Ciara would be like her and other pilgrims before them, who had found sustenance and new belief; the crazy and the lame, the poor and the half-believers, all of whom had travelled so far, so short a distance, and found home.

Nine Days:
Modes of Distraction

EVER SINCE WE LEFT COXSACKIE, we'd held to a tacit agreement not to talk about Rory. So I sat at the window, twisting for a better view of roofs and chimneys stretching across the sky and tried to sketch them. Blue merged to purple in the evening. Hunched at the end of the bed, I leant forward to delineate gardens which were tiny and packed in. A web, or warren, of green hedges. Our garden was tangled with dried grasses and red hot pokers clawing each other. My neck ached but in the distance the Wicklow Hills made a line of grey haze. In the street below, a man with a long ponytail pulled a shopping bag on wheels and two girls in short dresses clumped down the footpath.

In a new place I would have a studio like my old one, a garden of light flooding in, shelves for paints, canvases, brushes. I would work with the fury I used to have.

THE PAD'S SHEER WHITENESS, a hard purity like snow. Heavy falls lay around the house that February. Hills were crisp-topped and a cold wolf of wind nosed down the valley. White light teemed as Rory, snug as an airman, clutched my hand and we ventured out. He attempted to run, hobbling. Fell and sat like a fat alderman, declaring in a serious voice how he was tired. He scrambled up, spreading out his arms for support. We walked towards the lake. In the confusion of moving, it was possible some days to believe

Rory had tucked his two-year-old self among pots and pans in the kitchen cupboard. Dry air sank in my throat.

COLM PUSHED OPEN the bedroom door.

I'm back, he said as he sat on the bed. You're sickening for something. What are these? He pulled out the shiny packs, each label proclaiming: 0-3 months. Who are they for?

His face shadowed with puzzlement, eyebrows down, drawn together like a pair of caterpillars. The book with holes in the pages. How Rory had loved it and laughed. Holes through which singular sights were revealed. The fruit. The sun. The butterfly.

Silence fell into the hollowmost parts of me. Walls closed in on us. The dressing table and drawers.

I thought they'd be useful, I said.

We don't know anyone with a baby.

The sister of the girl in the next flat has three under five.

Is her sister here?

She lives in a village outside Kraków.

I lay the packs of baby-gros in the bottom drawer of the dressing table, the way babies were laid in poor families, years back. One outfit to wear. One in the wash and one spare.

Get shot of them or you'll be more upset.

He sighed.

Look, he said, don't you think we might try again? His arms, folded, drew me to the sofa. We have so much to give a child. And each other. He reached for my hand and held it in both of his and said, I wish things were as they were before. But we mustn't let what happened be an impediment.

The mirror caught my cheeks messed with tears, strands of hair awry. Loss stretched across my face in a thin, taut veil.

I'll return them, he said. Next time you're out, buy yourself something. You'll feel better.

He bundled the packages in his arms, smoothing out creases. He bent over and kissed me atop the head, picked up his backpack and went. He slammed shut the front door.

I WAS NOT MYSELF or any of the selves I had been. I pulled on a jacket, eager for air, and left. The next couple of days I wandered the network of tightly packed terraces with backyards so narrow it was a wonder washing lines could be strung across them. In a square, neat houses were hushed behind gardens with iron railings, but walking past they did not seem so cramped; rather they were tended to, cared for. A pale blue house at one end, with a flourish of tall flowers, looked peaceful and English. An expensive restaurant had opened. A Volvo garage swamped the corner and a florist had a vase of lavish, long-stemmed grasses in the window. Unprepared for so many changes, I had wanted Dun Laoghaire to be the same, to remind me of who I was, but it had changed in the years since I had gone. At the corner, two houses were being converted into a home for difficult children. Colm had called it a waste of the corporation's money but I liked the landscaping of the garden with low hedges and large glass doors.

I had wanted to live in the country after returning but Colm said he had to be near the university. I clicked on estate agents' websites. Red brick. Bay windows. Dormers. Other people's lives.

GREYSTONE VICTORIAN TERRACES ROSE UP, leading to an unfamiliar street of stark new houses and a block of flats. Cries came from a playground opposite. Usually I hurried, as though any minute Rory would waddle towards me. A girl in leggings and a pink T-shirt pushed a swing with her child in the boxy seat. Buggies crammed near the gate. The only accessory. The girl lit a cigarette, letting the swing go nonchalantly to and fro. The baby looked up, fat-cheeked and blooming. I could have swooped him into my arms, nuzzled him. The girl stubbed out her cigarette with her foot and hurried off. I wended away, past small houses backing onto one another until reaching the seafront, the sky opening up, a lighter grey and the wind squally and hard with its salty smell.

Boats clustered in the quay while plump gulls breasted the waves. Far out, a smudged pink sky was reflected in the water. Not like the sea of my childhood which flung waves madly at the shore. Rude and rough on winter nights, smooth and sheeny as glass in summer.

The path led along the cliff edge to the beach and the harbour. Wind tangled my hair and a boat far out had a red sail. Always someone sailing.

The main street had independent shops, like those in Coxsackie, where if I bought something, instead of online, I felt virtuous. A picture framer. A potter. Three cafés and two restaurants. A craft shop and several clothing boutiques. BELLE ISLE, I read above one shop with light summery tops and dresses in the window. Out of the sun, the shop was cool, discreet, but the clothes were colourful. Several orange and red dresses in light fabric hung on one rail. Another had tumbling dresses with ruffles and tiers.

A girl with short dark hair appeared beside me and asked if she could help.

Chiffon drifted under my fingers. I said, May I try this on?

In the changing room, the dress was a streak of light. As I turned side to side in the mirror it flashed and dazzled. Sleeveless with the armholes cut in, leaving my shoulders bare, it made me look boyish. Ethereal. Sophisticated. Grown up.

I pushed back the curtain. I'll take it, I said.

The girl smiled. It looks great.

I may as well wear it home.

Sure. I'll put your clothes in the bag instead.

I was lighter. Replenished. Filled with radiance. Birds called in the trees and traffic hummed. A line from a prayer of my mother's came to me: *This is today and we must praise it spilling its contents at our feet*. I had not understood at only seven years.

A SHOWER FILLED THE AIR. The red of the traffic lights was the same as those on the back of a car. Trees were dipped at the edges with light, from pale green to almost lemon. Nothing was staying the same. The clear day was sucked away as a leaden sky pressed down and unleashed rain. I should have taken an umbrella. The roads were liquorice strips. Hurrying, I reached a church on a corner and the heavy door fell open.

Velvet shadows. Light filtered through stained glass. A sulky angel in one window stood beside another in robes of whorish reds and purples. Lines of lead around the sections held in the colours. They glowed, alchemies of changing tones. Glass might be good to work with. Colours set, so they did not run.

I held a candle, an intense blue at the core while a flame curled around the outside as pale as the alb my brother had worn as an altar boy, supplicating himself at Easter. He had flown down, a bird in a little wind through the bleakness of Good Friday with the telling of what the soldiers did. The words of Pilate echoed: *What I have written, I have written*. Life was like this. What was done, was done. And the continual question resounded. Was Rory in heaven with saints and angels, with my grandmother who had walked miles to Mass? Or perhaps mouldering in the ground, chewed by worms and slugs? I had to believe he was in a safe place, even though Colm had given up on the proprieties of religion years ago, saying they had no logical foundation. Though rationally agreeing, I clung to a few tenets of faith, for belief beyond the confines of the tiny white coffin.

Excuse me?

A tall priest, his face unlined like a schoolboy's, smiled. Priests were strange creatures, seeming one thing and being another. Mercurial.

Are you here for the bazaar raffle? You wouldn't be Mrs. Fitzgerald? He shifted foot to foot and I wanted to leave. She's to meet me to give over the money raised, he said, but I'm new and haven't met all the parishioners.

I shook my head. Sorry. I came in out of the rain. Limp wet hair obscured my eyes.

Well, he said with a smile, we may as well use the roof over our heads.

A door at the back of the church scraped open. Straggling through was a fat, middle-aged woman with a soft hat and, hanging from the crook of an arm, a big shopping bag displaying the design of an assortment of flowers and the priest slipped off to greet her.

I LIKE BAD WEATHER. Droplets trickled down my neck through rats' tails of hair. I needed a cut, but couldn't remember the name of the girl who had done it last. At the bookshop on the corner, I grabbed the slippery door handle and tumbled into the warm premises.

Hiding amongst the shelves, I turned to photography books propped open. Except one. The cover. It chilled the insides of my bones. Him. Luke. He had slipped out of my consciousness. Behind the lettering, across the cover, were the gnarled backs of mountains and rivers and streams which ran over rocks riddled with gorse. I picked up the book, slipped through the pages of the outside world. Seas raged under the glossy texture as though under glass. A graze of green fields glowed from a height. One photograph showed a boat, with its worn, ruined wood taking up most of the frame. Here was the Moy, where Vivien Leigh's father had fished for salmon; there, the lake where Cúchulainn's sword had fallen.

A wide lens shot captured a row of severe peaks. Bare trees on a scraw hill, flecked with snow, electrified with distress. The land was scrubby, pure sparseness. Rivers and hills were sharply framed. Precipitous rocks ranged a scrabbled trail down sharp cliffs, where the only alternative was the gaping, charging sea as birds darted and gulls dived for food. Otherwise, beyond creatures of the deep, no other living thing survived.

As a kind of companion, for night, I bought the book. A reflection in the door met me on leaving. Ragged hair. It did not matter. Nothing did, for the bag with the book hung and swung with my movements. The book, trapped. His words caught. On the pavement a sign said BREAKFAST ALL DAY. I did not know how this could be. But of course it was possible even as threads of time were out of kilter, slipping sideways.

ABBA BLASTED FROM A RETRO TV SHOW when I came in. Colm rose and placed his laptop on the kitchen table. You didn't take your phone, he said. His eyes, dark, flayed. The whole of the afternoon had fallen away behind us. The clock said twenty past six. Colm murmured, I thought I'd come home early. I got a good bottle of wine. He brandished the bottle with a particularly delicate label of pinks and blues.

Home? Where was this?

But you clearly forgot to buy the fish, Colm added. He held the fridge door open.

I'm sure there's food, I said. I reached for a cupboard and glanced along the kitchen counter, as though to miraculously encounter a haddock or plaice, pure white flesh glistening on a plate.

Oh, he said, there's food, but the trouble is it's not cooked. I'd better go around the corner and get a takeaway. Chicken chow mein?

He didn't wait for an answer and I wanted to run out after him, calling, It doesn't matter. I don't care. But gravity grabbed my ankles and I sank to the sofa.

When he came back, he laid the packages of rice and chicken on the kitchen counter and we divided the dishes. We sat to eat while rain spattered the windows which misted with the heat of our breathing.

LUKE'S VOICE BLED IN, descriptions of streams and mountains. The confluence of paths over rough stones weathered with moss and lichen. He brought back how he had lived. Amongst woods. Along streams, at the edges of the sea. He had disturbed my heart more than a decade before. We had driven to Dingle, slept on a beach for a week in August, his head resting on my belly, days and night bleeding together. We drove one rainy morning to the magnificence of the Cliffs of Moher. I had been alarmed, bracing against a biting wind. While rain lashed us both he stood in awe of the elements. He had been easy to be with. Or mostly. His years over mine were a type of hold. He used to ring late at night, saying he was calling round, and I acceded to him and the long mornings.

Restless to be outdoors, he had sought the open air and we had walked miles in full winds, jackets making us fat, our mouths seeking one another's. He opened up the outer world, explaining how features derived from phenomena. A glacial valley: its steep sides fell in a drop to a floor as wide as a palace ballroom.

YOU THERE? Colm called through the bedroom door and thumped down his bag. I flipped shut the book and shoved it under the bed. You remembered flowers for the party, he said. But they'll have cost a bomb. Delphiniums, carnations, and lilies stretched their heads. And you've used the bucket.

We're short of vases, I said. But aren't they lovely?

The vase on the mantelpiece held a clutch of creamy orchids. Shadows of stark green stippled over. I breathed in. Summers. My parents' garden had been vibrant with lupins, foxgloves. Dizzying scents.

You've lots of friends here, I said.

Exactly. You need to meet people. If you saw a doctor, he could give you something. Help you get out of yourself.

He'd cut his ginger hair so short, the vibrancy of his curls was gone. A vase of fiery peonies glowed behind him. He was right. The flat was overstuffed. The confusion of our accumulated possessions stacked and toppled in every room. Fragile towers of art materials, table lamps, chairs from the front porch, rugs made by craftspeople we'd known. The sediment and debris of a shared life on another continent. The olive eyes of the Argentinian psychotherapist had pierced me. He was a tiny man whose long arms and lithe movements reminded me of a lizard. I did not want to talk to a stranger. Talking made the loss expand inside, so I was larger with the weight of expectation, the expectation of things improving. And dashed when they did not.

COLM LEANT IN CLOSE to stroke my hair.

Soon you'll get back to painting, he said. In a routine. It won't be like last time.

Last time was the last time with Rory. For all time. And it was my fault. His flighty blonde hair in the lake under the crack of glassy ice. A man had gone out in a boat. Too late. Always too late. Rory lay on the ground, cheeks murky and softened with earth. Soils spilt from his mouth and his eyes were closed. Blue as petals. Cornflowers. His face was pale, delicate, with fine veins of lavender. At the side of his head, blood trickled from the impact of a rock. Gritty texture had imprinted his skin. I had clutched him, unable to fathom why having borne him I could not now give him new life.

THE DARK TONES of the kitchen counter and the metallic fridge were like my uncle's butcher shop: cabinets big enough to walk into and flashes of chunky red flesh hanging from hooks, thick with blood and melting white tissue. The radio forecast hot weather. Spanish weather, my father had called it, though he had never been to Spain. Never even fifty miles from the farm. He must have been thinking of the phrase from the song:

> First she washed them, then she dried them
> Over a fire of amber coals
> In all my life I ne'er did see
> A maid so sweet about the soul...

A sole? A person's foot. Or their soul? The lady's or someone else's? It would have been unusual for my father to sing words riven with confusion, for he was level-headed, practical, with skills of carpentry. A man who knew his own business, making tables and dressers and mending everything: a lopsided chair, the runner for a drawer. He made things new. If only I could put on a new skin, start life over again. Wasn't this meant to happen every seven years? All I had to do was wait to become a new person.

Acknowledgements

Acknowledgements are due to Honno Press, *The Southern Review*, Liars League, London, the Word Factory, *Matador*, Cork Library Service, and The Lonely Crowd. Thank you Daniel Davis Wood and Alec Dewar of Splice. Particular thanks are due to Daniel for his assiduous editing. Thank you Tessa Hadley, Cathy Galvin, Billy O'Callaghan for selecting my work at various times. Thank you Ludo Cinelli for critical feedback on earlier drafts. As ever, thank you Jonathan for holding the fort while I have been away with the stories.